THE MISCREANT

JEAN COCTEAU

THE MISCREANT

Translated from the French by
DOROTHY WILLIAMS

PETER OWEN
LONDON AND CHESTER SPRINGS

PETER OWEN LTD
73 Kenway Road, London SW5 0RE

Peter Owen books are distributed in the USA by
Dufour Editions Inc., Chester Springs, PA 19425-0007

Translated from the French *Le Grand Ecart*

First British Commonwealth edition 1958
© Peter Owen and Dorothy Williams 1958
This paperback edition 2003

A catalogue record for this book is available from
the British Library

ISBN 0 7206 1173 3

Printed and bound in Great Britain by
Bookmarque Ltd, Croydon, Surrey

Of all my books, *The Miscreant* is the one that dates, and that is deliberate. I mean in which the period is caught, cruelly pinned to a cork like the entomologist's butterfly. Besides, I liked substituting swift significant anecdotes for argument and voluminous studies, threaded on the red string of love—on a unifying action, action which would bring out the awful loneliness of youth—but of a youth carried away by his relationships.

My whole work hangs on the drama of loneliness and man's attempts to overcome it. It is shown here without contrivances (except those of my youthful accomplices), and, as it were, utterly naked.

I

Jacques Forestier cried easily. Films, bad music, a romantic serial, would bring tears to his eyes. He did not confuse these deceptive signs of softheartedness with deep tears. These seemed to come to his eyes for no reason.

As he hid his shallow tears in the darkness of a theatre box or alone with a book, he was considered an insensitive and witty man.

He had a reputation for wit because his mind was sharp. He would take rhymes from the four winds and link them in such a way that they seemed to have rhymed always. By rhymes, we mean: anything at all.

He would force the meaning of proper nouns, faces, actions, and diffident suggestions to extremes. This behaviour earned him a reputation for lying.

He also admired handsome figures and faces, regardless of their sex. Because of this last peculiarity he was given credit for loose living; this being the only thing for which credit is given without forethought.

As Jacques' appearance was not all he would have desired, and did not conform with his own ideal type of young man, he stopped trying to live up to the ideal which was too far from him. He exaggerated his weak points, mannerisms and ridiculous ways until they were no longer liabilities. He deliberately brought them out.

Through tilling barren soil, forcing and improving weeds, he had acquired a hard streak that was quite inconsistent with his gentleness.

He had been slim; he deliberately became thin: he had been nervous; he made his nerves raw. As his bristly, yellow hair was difficult to control, he kept it untidy. Besides, an appearance as artificial as possible, gave him the advantages of artifice, hiding a bourgeois love of order, the unhealthy detachment which he inherited from his father, and his mother's melancholia.

If one of the skilful, ferocious Parisian huntsmen dislodged him, it was easy to wring his neck. He could be demoralized with a single word.

*   *   *

Out of contempt for the simple superiority which

consists in running counter to the spirit of one's class, Jacques adopted the spirit of his; but in him it took such a different form his equals could not recognize it as their own.

In short, he was handsome in a suspicious way: like an animal. This aristocrat, this son of the people, who could not bear the aristocracy or the masses deserved the Bastille and guillotine a dozen times a day. He was not satisfied with the right or the left, which he thought weak. Only his extremist nature could see no golden mean.

In accordance with the axiom: *extremes meet*, he dreamt of a virgin extreme right so close to the extreme left that it almost merged with it—but where he could act independently. The chair would not exist, but if it did, it would be unoccupied. Jacques nominated himself to take it, and from that seat he surveyed all politics, art and behaviour.

He was not trying to engineer a reward. That provokes censure.

From schemers, because detachment brings a certain good luck which they could not admit to be independent of intrigue. From those who give the reward, because they are never asked for it.

To get on. Jacques wondered where successful people get to. Did Napoleon get to the Coronation or

St. Helena? Does a train get anywhere if it makes a sensation by running off the lines and killing the passengers? Does it get further if it reaches the station?

A closer search for a profile of Jacques leads me to denounce him as a parasite on earth.

Indeed, where was the document that authorized him to enjoy a meal, a fine evening, a girl or men? Let him show it. All society confronts him like a civil servant and demands it. He is confused. He stammers. He cannot find it.

This pleasure-seeker whose feet were planted firmly on the ground, this critic of scenery and man-made things was holding on to the earth by a single thread.

He was as heavy as a diver.

Jacques dug around on the bottom. He could sense it. He had acclimatized himself to it. No-one brought him up to the surface again. They had forgotten him. To come up, to take the helmet and the suit off was to pass from life to death. But a breath of illusion blew down the tube, bringing him to life and overwhelming him with nostalgia.

*　　　　*　　　　*

Jacques spent his life struggling with one long fit of fainting. He felt unstable. He built no foundations except for amusement. He hardly dared sit down. He was the kind of sailor who cannot get over his sea-sickness.

*   *   *

Beauty which is strictly physical has an assuming, arrogant manner of being at home everywhere. Exiled, Jacques coveted it. The less desirable it was, the more it affected him; for it was his fate to be hurt by it always.

He saw a dance through the windows: the race who have their papers in order, who are glad to be alive, in their proper element, with no use for diving suits.

So he wove dreams around unkind faces.

*   *   *

This is what the ideal graphologist would learn from the handwriting of Jacques Forestier who is now studying himself in his wardrobe mirror.

Make no mistake. We have just drawn Jacques in full face, but even here we have no more than a profile of his character. That is why we were speaking of an ideal graphologist. In disentangling the strokes of the pen, he would have to disentangle the whole line of a life. Jacques will become the man who precedes partly as a result of what is to follow; and what is to follow will happen partly as a result of what precedes.

*   *   *

Objects and atoms take their business seriously. If the mirror were not concentrating, Jacques could doubtless put in one leg and then the other, until he was standing at a vital angle so new as to be inconceivable. No. The mirror was playing safe. The mirror was a mirror. The wardrobe a wardrobe. The room a room, on the second floor, rue de l'Estrapade.

He was still thinking of the Englishman who committed suicide having written: *too many buttons to do up and undo, I'm killing myself.* For Jacques was unbuttoning his jacket.

Waiting. What was he waiting for? Jacques would have liked to have been waiting for something definite, to simplify the wait. He did not believe, or his belief took such a muddled form that his mother prayed for him, considering him an atheist.

Having a vague belief makes minds dilettante. He believed too much. He did not limit his beliefs nor define them. Limiting one's beliefs fixes a spiritual attitude just as defining and limiting one's tastes in art fixes an attitude of mind.

*   *   *

He studied himself. He inflicted the sight on himself.

14

---

*   *   *

We are full of things which make us hate ourselves. Since his childhood he had longed to be one of those whom he thought handsome and not to be loved for it by them. He did not like his own good looks. He thought he was ugly.

Memories of human beauty stayed with him like wounds. One evening at Mürren, for example. At the foot of the mountains, visitors gulp down cold beer that shoots directly to the head and blows it to smithereens. The cable car moves off through the blackberry bushes. Their ears are gradually blocked, their noses clear; they have arrived.

Jacques was eleven years old. He remembered a priest who had lost his trunk, being half-asleep, the hotel with its sweet smell of resin, their grimy arrival in the lounge where the ladies were playing patience, the men smoking and reading the papers. Suddenly as they stopped in front of the lift-shaft, the lift came down and dropped a couple. A young man and a girl with dark faces and starry eyes, laughing and displaying magnificent teeth. The girl was wearing a blue dress with a blue belt. The boy was dressed for dinner. There was a clatter of crockery and a foul smell of cooking in the corridors.

Once in his room, which looked out on to a wall of ice, Jacques looked at himself. He compared himself to the couple. He would gladly have died.

Later he got to know the young pair. Tigrane d'Ybreo, the son of an Armenian from Cairo, collected stamps and concocted sickly sweets over a spirit lamp. His sister Idgi wore new dresses and dilapidated shoes. They used to dance together.

The dilapidated shoes and the honey cakes denoted a royal but sordid race. Jacques dreamt of this cooking and the holes. He desired them. He saw in them the only means of identifying himself with these two sacred cats. He wanted to collect stamps, make almond toffees. He wore his tennis pumps out by an artificial method.

Idgi was always coughing. She was tubercular. Tigrane broke his leg skating. Their father used to receive telegrams. One morning they went away coughing and limping, followed by a dog as mysterious as Anubis.

Jacques coughed. His mother was desperately worried. He let her suffer for him. He was coughing for love. On the road he would limp when no one was looking.

Every evening after dinner, when he sat in the straw-bottomed chair, he fancied he could see Idgi, in her Virgin Mary dress, framed in the lighted lift between the pageboy and Tigrane, as she was borne up by angels into heaven.

From eleven to eighteen years old, he burnt himself up, like the Armenian paper that flares up quickly and has an unpleasant smell.

Finally, the journeys to Switzerland came to an end. Mme Forestier took him from the Italian lakes to Venice.

*　　　*　　　*

By Lake Maggiore he met a student teacher who was annotating Bergson and Taine. He had a fair moustache, an eye-glass and his humour was a parody of Barres'. His intellect was sharp. He savoured it like a barley sugar as he wore it away. This undisciplined disciple thought nothing of the Borromean Islands. He nicknamed them *"The Isola sisters."*

This witticism was Jacques' first revelation of how freely the senses can be used. He accepted these islands without investigation.

*　　　*　　　*

By day, Venice is the shattered pieces of an ornate shooting-range on a fairground. By night, she is an amorous negress lying dead in her bath with her tawdry jewels.

On the night of their arrival, the hotel gondola is as entertaining as a fairground amusement. It is no ordinary vehicle. Unhappily, parents do not see it that way. Venice begins the next day. Tonight they do not take a gondola; they take a bus. They count the trunks. The town is like the Opera, backstage; they do not look at it.

The following morning, Jacques saw the crowd of tourists. Trapped in the theatrical setting of the square of St. Mark, this fashionable crowd discloses every secret it has, as it might at a masked ball. The most immodest frankness overrides age and sex. The shyest finally venture the gesture or the dress which they hardly dared contemplate in London or Paris.

The masked ball is certainly revealing. It might be a medical board. With her footlights and spotlights Venice lays hearts bare.

For Jacques, the pangs of love were to take a more deceptive turn than at Mürren. As he lay under his mosquito net, at night, he could hear guitars, tenors. He suspected clandestine meetings. He cried because he was not the town. Heliogabalus, in his wildest flights of fancy, demanded no more.

The student from Baveno was passing through

Venice. He introduced Jacques to a young journalist
and a dancer. They often went out together.

One night when the journalist was going back with
Jacques as far as his hotel, he said:

"I live a vile life in Paris. I am in love with this girl
who hasn't a suspicion of it. When I go back, I can't
possibly continue my old relationships, and on the
other hand I know I shall find it very hard to break
them off."

"But . . . if Bertha is in love with you?" (this was
the dancer's name).

"Oh! She doesn't love me. You ought to know that.
In any case, I intend to kill myself in two hours."

Jacques jokingly reminded him of the classic suicide
of Venice and wished him good night.

The journalist committed suicide. The dancer was
in love with Jacques. He had not seen it and only
came to know of it years later through a third person.

This episode left him disgusted with the nauseating
poetry of disease. He still had an intermittent fever
caught on a walk in the Eaden Garden which was an
unpleasant reminder of his stay.

*   *   *

Mme Forestier was afraid of colds, bronchitis and
motor accidents. She did not distinguish spiritual

---

dangers. She let Jacques play with them.

*   *   *

Venice had disappointed Jacques like a stage set that is warped with use, because every performer erects it for at least one act of his life.

After two hours of walking and concentrating in the museums, the splendour fell on his shoulders like a dead weight.

Half-dead with exhaustion and cramp, he came out, went down the steps, saw the palazzo Dario bowing to the boxes in front like an old singer, and returned to his hotel. He admired the vigour of the couples who go round Venice with insect-like activity. Those who know her by heart and have dipped their trumpets hundreds of times before into the golden pollen of Saint Mark show their new sweethearts round the square. This Ciceronian role rejuvenates them. They only pause to sit down in a shop, where the object of their affections buys glass jewellery, volumes of Wilde and D'Annunzio.

Stimulated by his slight fever, Jacques, like us when we recall it, was filled with mounting distaste for this charming brothel where the rarest spirits slake their thirst.

Our very insistence proves how far he had succumbed to a spell which his dark side repelled.

*　　　*　　　*

Half dark, half light: this is the way of the planets. One half of the world rests, the other works. But from the half that is dreaming, there emanates a mysterious strength.

In man, the sleeping half contradicts the active. It is the voice of nature itself.

If the lesson bears fruit, the man listens and puts his light side in order, the dark side will grow dangerous. Its rôle will change. It will give out poisonous fumes. We are to see Jacques struggling with this night of the body.

For the time being it was protecting him, providing him with antidotes, files and rope-ladders.

*　　　*　　　*

All help does not achieve its end. Paris is a more cunning town than Venice, in the sense that its pitfalls are better hidden and its equipment is not so simple. You know in advance with Venice, as with certain houses, that there is water, the chamber of mirrors, the Veronese room, the Bridge of Sighs, weary beauties in pink petticoats, and the danger of infection.

You can hardly recognise yourself in Paris.

Jacques, the Parisian, the privileged, returned to Paris from the provinces.

He had come from there five months before, but on the way he had crossed the narrow borderline to the age at which the mind and the body can choose.

His mother thought she was bringing back the same person, rather disturbed by the panoramas of Italv. She was bringing back another person. And it was precisely in Venice that the change had occurred. Jacques only felt it through his uneasiness. He attributed that to the suicide and the unexpected meetings at night in the arcades. In reality, he was leaving a dry skin floating on the Grand Canal, like a snake's slough hanging on a wild rose bush, as light as foam, slit at the eyes and mouth.

II

The map of our life is folded in such a way that we cannot see one main road across it, but as it is opened out, we are constantly seeing new side roads. We think we are choosing, and we have no choice.

*   *   *

A young Persian gardener said to his Prince:

"I met death this morning. She made me a sign of warning. Save me. By some miracle I should like to be in Ispahan tonight." The good Prince lent him his horses. That afternoon, the Prince met death.

"Why did you make a sign of warning at our gardener this morning?" he asked.

"I did not make a sign of warning but a sign of surprise," she answered. "For this morning I saw him far from Ispahan, and I am to take him in Ispahan tonight."

* * *

Jacques was working for his baccalauréat. His parents, obliged to live in Touraine for a year after the loss of a perfect bailiff, sent him to M. Berlin's boarding school in the rue de l'Estrapade.

M. Berlin rented two floors. He kept the first to himself and put the boarders together on the second, five rooms off a sordid corridor, lit by a gas burner so encrusted with dirt that it would not turn full on.

Jacques' room was between those of Mouheddin Bashtarzi, the son of a rich merchant from Saint-Eugene, which is the Auteuil of Algiers, and of an albino: Pierre de Maricelles. A very young boy with a weak but engaging face lived opposite. He answered to the pseudonym of Petitcopain.

The year before, in the Sologne, he and his younger brother had wanted to play a trick on their tutor. But just as they were going to enter his room at midnight, dressed up as ghosts, the door opened, and their mother came out in her night-gown, with her hair rumpled. They were hidden by the door. She crossed the hall, put her ear to their father's door, and returned to the tutor's room without seeing them.

Petitcopain was never to forget the moment when they got back into bed without saying a word.

*　　　*　　　*

The last room was chaos. There in the flotsam of text books, exercise books, ties, shirts, pipes, ink, tubs, sponges, fountain pens, handkerchiefs and blankets, camped Peter Stopwell, long jump champion.

*　　　*　　　*

Mme Berlin was far more sprightly than her husband, left a widower after his first marriage. She simpered and thought that the boys were in love with her. Occasionally she would go into one of their rooms, where the boy would be standing in a stupid position after rushing to hide some occupation unconnected with his work. She would look the reddening boy up and down, and burst out laughing.

She would declaim Racine in places where it is appropriate to be quiet. One day, when she realised that she was caught out, the boys heard her change her oration into a cough which gradually lapsed into silence.

One significant feature of Mme Berlin was this. When they were first married in the country, Berlin and she had taken in a lodger, a divorced woman who was a pianist. Berlin came home on the seven o'clock train

every evening after college. One evening he had to
stay in town. Mme Berlin, who was very frightened,
begged the pianist to sleep near her. The pianist
made the best of it and moved into the family bed.
Berlin slept out twice in one week, and his wife put
her question again. The pianist wished her bed-fellow
good night, turned to the wall, and returned quickly
to her room the following morning.

Seven years later, when a group of people were talking about the pianist, all accusing her of having
doubtful morals, Mme Berlin smiled mysteriously and
declared that to judge from her personal experience
she had every reason to believe that the woman absolutely flaunted her vices.

She was a naïve actress, hoping for example to take
in her guests when she served the tea lukewarm by
pretending to burn her tongue.

"Don't drink!" she would cry. "Wait! It's boiling!"

Berlin surveyed his wife, his boys, and life with
lack-lustre eyes behind pince-nez.

He wore a white beard and slippers. He had trousers
like the man acting the hind legs of an elephant at the
circus. He taught at the Sorbonne, played cards in the
café Voltaire and came home to sleep. His pupils took
advantage of his sleepiness to recite whatever they
liked.

Stopwell and Petitcopain:
This love flattered Stopwell.

The maid completes the picture. There was never the same one. They were changed every fortnight, generally because they dusted a Boule clock which M. Berlin always wound up himself and allowed no one else to touch.

At midday and eight o'clock they all met for a meal at which Mme Berlin served out leathery meat.

Her husband ate mechanically. Now and then he would be shaken by a gloomy hiccup which made him quiver like a mountain of snow.

*   *   *

Peter Stopwell would have had the beauty of a Greek if the long jump had not drawn him out like a photograph taken from the wrong angle. He had just come down from Oxford. Hence his fatuity, his boxes of cigarettes, his navy blue muffler, and the multiform immorality beneath the sportsman's uniform. Petit-copain loved him.

On Sundays, he carried a bag containing the sports clothes and the towelling wrap to the Parc des Princes.

To love and be loved, that is the ideal. Providing, of course, that the same person is involved. The opposite often happens. Petitcopain was in love and he was loved. Only he had a student in a laboratory in love with him and he was in love with Stopwell. His love stupefied him.

He was a victim of the half-light where the senses meet the emotions.

This love flattered Stopwell. He showed no sign of it. He snapped at the poor child.

"That is not done," he would say in response to the slightest childish caresses. Or;

"You are not clean, you know. Wash yourself. Have a bath. Rub yourself down. You never have a bath. If you don't bath, you will *smell*."

Stopwell's rebukes were often a kind of English teasing. But Petitcopain knew nothing but the ABC of laughter and tears. He did not understand. He thought he was dirty, wicked, and stupid.

One evening when Petitcopain, seated on the edge of the bed where Peter Stopwell was smoking, put his hand religiously on his shoulder, Stopwell pushed him away and asked him if he was a girl to hang round men's necks.

Petitcopain dissolved into tears.

"Oh, you are always begging things of me, crying, touching me, petting me," said Stopwell, lighting a cigarette from the stub which he threw carelessly away.

"You'd do better to go out with girls. You can find ones for sixpence behind the Pantheon."

*　　　*　　　*

Maricelles was the sixth son of a family of delicate country squires. Constipation kept this albino endlessly in a place which he made inaccessible. With the Maricelles it was the rule that patience alone must solve such problems, the youngest brother having died of a ruptured aneurism for having tried to force fate.

"You love dirt, you French," said Stopwell to Petitcopain. "Molière talks about nothing but purges."

Petitcopain hung his head and did not dare go through that ridiculous door.

*　　　*　　　*

Mouheddin Bashtarzi, of Turkish extraction, sported the tarbush. He owned one in red, one in soft grey fur and one in astrakhan. He was big, fat, puerile. His visiting cards bore the strange inscription:

MOUHEDDIN BASHTARZI
Inspector

He wrote poems, inhaled ether. One day when the smell of ether was growing too strong, Jacques went into his room and found him sitting on the sill of the open window with his tarbush on his head, slavering and holding his left nostril with one hand and putting

33

a medicine bottle to the right nostril with the other. Not hearing Jacques he was swaying, deafened by the cicadas that were frozen by the drug.

Was that the ideal environment in the mind of a delicate mother, afraid of germs and draughts?

*   *   *

After a few difficult days Jacques had just settled into the Berlin place, when a tragi-comical interlude broke the peace. Petitcopain fell ill, in such a way that there could be no doubt as to the cause of his pains.

M. Berlin got the truth from him. He learnt that the poor child had taken Stopwell's advice literally. Petitcopain was sobbing.

"It's unbelievable," cried Mme Berlin. "But the story ought not to be spread."

Jacques went to see him every day. One evening, in an expressionless voice, Petitcopain begged him to ask Peter why he had never come to his room.

Stopwell was annotating Auguste Comte, in a haze.

"Why, simply because he disgusts me," he said. "Do you think I would want to see a boy who sleeps with diseased women. *I* don't sleep with anyone."

"You are hard," murmured Jacques. "The poor child; he is not asking much . . ."

"Not much! What if my regiment could see me with him fiddling about with my hands. I think you must be going mad."

His "what if my regiment could see me?" sounded like a girl saying, "what if my mother could see me?"

Jacques was preparing to go when Peter pulled him back by the sleeve, opening a box of cigarettes.

"What? Are you going back to that ape? At Oxford, we treat them like servants. Leave him alone and stay with me."

His hand was gripping Jacques with herculean strength. He made him sit down on his trunk.

Was his gesture enough to remove a mask? Roses lose their flawless cheeks in the same way once we have struck the vase. Jacques saw a new face, utterly naked, without a trace of composure.

He rose.

"No, Stopwell, it's late," he said, "I have to write a letter."

"Just as you like, old man."

With the skill of a trickster Stopwell turned round to show a face repaired, a new mask, supported by a cigarette.

*　　　　*　　　　*

In short Petitcopain did not like Jacques, being jealous of the pretended favours bestowed on him.

Stopwell loathed Petitcopain and deliberately misled him. Bashtarzi resented him for having come in while he was inhaling ether. Maricelles despised the whole lot of them.

There remained the Berlin family.

Occasionally at mealtimes a pertinent remark from Jacques would bring a light to the master's eye and Mme Berlin appointed as supervisor by her husband would always stay longer in his room than in the others. She did not think Stopwell a "gentleman." The Arab "frightened" her. The others were children.

One Saturday night when all the boys had gone out either to their families or to the theatre, Jacques, who had a sore throat, was left all alone on that floor. Mme Berlin brought him some herbal tea, felt his forehead and his pulse. Jacques soon saw that the mistress of the house was playing Stopwell's game; but this time instead of his coldness being enough to quench the flames, it was fanning them, and Mme Berlin was unconsciously abandoning the rôle of second mother.

Jacques pretended not to understand, and while he coughed, moaning like an invalid trying to sleep, he watched Mme Berlin through his eyelids, a Mme Berlin driven mad by desire, just as her shadow was driven by the candle to left and to right against the walls of the room.

Germaine

In the end, with an amazing grip she grabbed his hand.

"Jacques, Jacques, what are you doing then?" she murmured.

The sound of a side-door saved him. Mme Berlin let go, put herself straight and rushed out.

Mouheddin was coming back from the theatre. Jacques heard him whistling a popular song. He went wrong and repeated the mistake.

The following day at mealtime Jacques did not dare look at Mme Berlin. She, on the other hand, faced him bravely, reassured him, forgave him.

*　　　　*　　　　*

Jacques was living in complete solitude, and working like a real slacker. What did he know? Nothing. Only that our every movement brings us into conflict with our fellow men. He would gladly have died of his sore throat. But he had almost stopped coughing.

Mouheddin suggested that they should go to the Scala together. You can get a stage box very cheaply for the matinées on Sundays and Thursdays. Jacques tried to be pleasant. He agreed. They lured Petitcopain. He received nice little sums of money from his family who lived in the North.

In this way, on the third Sunday, Jacques met

Mouheddin's mistress: Louise Champagne.

Louise was better known than her dancing and had a better position in the demi-monde than on the theatre bills. She was one of the women who make two pounds at the theatre and two thousand at home. She told Jacques that he could not live alone and that she would find him a friend: Germaine.

This popular girl played four parts in the revue which was ready to flop exhausted after three hundred and fifty performances.

Germaine smiled high up between the orchestra and the drum. Her beauty was near ugliness, but in the same way as an acrobat is near death. It was a way of arousing emotion.

This black and white attracted Jacques.

Unfortunately the kind of liberty we enjoy allows us to misbehave in a way which plants and animals avoid. With Louise's lamp Jacques felt his desire again.

After the first contact in her dressing-room, Louise took on the final arrangements and asked Jacques to go and see her at her home in the rue Montchanin.

The following day he cut his lessons, as schoolboys say, left Mouheddin there and ran to the place where they were to meet-

*   *   *

He found Champagne crestfallen. Germaine did not like him. She thought him attractive. He was not her type.

Louise felt sad to have to pass on bad news.

"Poor little thing!"

She stroked the back of his neck, tweaked his nose, in short openly offered to console him.

Peter, Mme Berlin, well and good. It was growing more difficult to refuse. Louise Champagne was beautiful and there was no way of getting off the sofa. They deceived the Arab.

Bashtarzi had no suspicions and cursed Germaine, for she had a larger car than Louise's little runabout, and Mouheddin already saw a harem life ahead of him.

One Sunday Jacques was walking backstage past Germaine's dressing room. She called him, shut him in, and asked him why he had backed out after the steps Louise had taken and her own favourable reply and gone so far as to make Louise behave as rudely as himself.

Jacques was amazed. Germaine saw that his amazement was not pretended, talked him round, consoled him, and stopped speaking to Louise.

On the pretext that he loathed to deceive Mouheddin, Jacques followed up his new conquest. Louise went to Mouheddin and accused Jacques of having made advances to her. She refused to see him.

The neighbours in the rue de l'Estrapade lived as strangers to one another.

III

In Paris, art, especially the worst, removes stains like magic. It does not wash them out, it mounts them. From then on a bad reputation, given top billing, is as useful as a good one. It needs to be as carefully guarded. Many kept women use the stage to make them immune. The theatre is a tax they pay, but it interferes with their work.

After the theatre treatment, Germaine and Louise gave themselves a holiday. They made it a long one. They did not make a living out of art.

Germaine had a rich lover, so rich that his name alone meant wealth. He was called Nestor Osiris, like a box of cigarettes. Lazare his brother kept Loute, Germaine's younger sister.

Germaine was loving and would gladly have sent Osiris to the devil, but her sister was thinking of the future.

She disapproved of Jacques. Although she herself had deceived Lazare with a painter she knew that her sister would not play the trick cautiously and was afraid of the consequences.

She was as much like Germaine as a plaster cast is to the original marble. That is to say they were alike, except in every way.

*   *   *

In spite of the abominable air Jacques had been breathing since his seizure his heart was still in a state of innocence and capable of an ideal love.

*   *   *

Germaine's bloom came from the manure heap. She fed on it as greedily as a rose; and while the rose presents the picture of a long mouth sucking up perfume from the dead, her laugh, her lips and cheeks owed their brightness to the failures of the Bourse.

*   *   *

The indifference of a landscape gives us every opportunity of sneering at it. Had Venice offered

44

*Loute: That is to say that they were alike,
except in every way.*

itself, would Jacques have sneered at Venice?

*   *   *

The heart lives in confinement. Hence its outbursts of melancholy, its fits of deep despair. Ever ready to pour out its riches, it is at the mercy of its membrane. What does it know, the poor blind thing? It watches anxiously for the slightest sign that would relieve the tedium. Thousands of nerves bring the news. Is the object for which its help is sought a worthy one? It does not matter. It pours itself out trustingly, it drains itself dry and if it is ordered to stop it writhes and gasps out its last.

Jacques' heart had just been told to start. It did so with a beginner's clumsiness and enthusiasm.

So Jacques was afraid of the first effects of the capsule which opens inside us and releases a powerful drug.

As quickly as a tiny woman in a group on the cinema screen is followed by the woman's face in close-up six times life size, Germaine's face filled the world, concealed the future and hid from Jacques not only his examinations and his friends but his mother, his father, himself. All around, darkness prevailed. This darkness also concealed Osiris.

There is a story in which children sew stones into

47

the stomach of a sleeping wolf. When he awoke, Jacques felt an unknown weight, an unsteadiness that could have drowned him like the wolf as it bent over the water to drink.

Without a doubt, Germaine loved him. But her little heart was no beginner. It was not an equal match.

At the circus, a careless mother may let her child take part in the experiments of a Chinese magician. He puts him in a box. He opens the box; it is empty. He closes it again. He opens it; the child reappears and goes back to its seat. Now it is no longer the same child. Nobody doubts it.

*   *   *

One Sunday Jacques saw his mother. She came to collect him at the boarding school. How could she sense his recent metamorphosis, after failing to realise that she had brought a changed son back from Venice? She thought he looked well, but rather thin. She was translating his exhaustion and burning cheeks into maternal language.

Mme Forestier was short-sighted and lived in the past: two reasons which prevented her from forming an accurate idea of present things. In her son she worshipped the resemblance to a grandmother, in her husband the father of Jacques. She appeared cold because she carried her scruples so far as to form no liaisons, being afraid of what she called infatuations. Her only friend was dead. Her life was divided between the Church, her husband, who was a good one, and her fears for Jacques' future.

Alone with him, she harassed him with tender criticism, but in front of strangers or her husband, she heaped praise on him.

If we leave M. Forestier in the background it is because he himself kept in the background. When he was young he suffered from a demon similar to the one that tortured Jacques. He kept it down by study and marriage. But a demon is difficult to keep down. His upright nature was atrophied. It felt that it had been bent. Now M. Forestier guessed what was disturbing Jacques, and recognising it, he was as dismayed as a man with a sarcoma in his shoulder which has been cured, who feels the pain start again in his knee.

"So are you feeling well, Jacques?" said his mother.

"Yes, mother."

"Are you working?"

"Yes, mother."

"Your friends?"

"Nothing special. An Arab, an Englishman and two youngsters."

"You should take the opportunity of living with an Englishman to learn his language."

This sentence took Jacques so far from reality that he did not reply. He was usually glad to go shopping with his mother, but he now felt that the time they spent together was time wasted.

Deception irritated him, enveloped everything in a stifling atmosphere of artificiality. As he could not tell his mother about Germaine, he would have preferred her to go away, so that she would not force him to keep his distance from her.

He was in love.

He did not want to be Germaine. He wanted to possess her. For the first time his desire did not manifest itself in the form of a sick feeling. For the first time, he did not hate his own reflection. He thought he was cured.

The vague longing for beauty is death to us.

We have explained how Jacques was wearing himself out with desire for thin air. Surely the figures and faces unmoved by our wild glances are thin air.

This time the desire met a sensitive surface, and Germaine's response was the very reflection of Jacques, just as the screen releases the film which, if there were no barrier, would only spread out in a white sheaf. Jacques saw himself in this desire, and for the first time he was overwhelmed at meeting himself. In Germaine, he loved himself. He became unconscious of the character he would develop later, without trying to live up to his ideal.

Until then the women who liked him were not the ones he liked. He knew their weak profiles. All the heads in the world can be put into a few categories. He knew in advance that certain high-bosomed brunettes would fall in love with him.

Germaine did not belong to the generation of great intimidating girls with the same names as race horses. But there was something unattainable, supernatural about her, the thing which can turn the sailor on the quay at Naples or a tennis player at Houlgate into a memory of unhappiness.

So one of the thousands of passers-by had stopped. He had caught him in his trap. In him he would love all streets, all towns on his first night there, the disturbing temperature of ports, Idgi and Tigrane d'Ybreo, the jackal dog, the troop of acrobats in Geneva and the circus rider in Rome.

He thought of these things uninterruptedly until the train left, taking Mme Forestier to Tours.

IV

"Now don't worry, Loute," said Germaine to her sister. "Nestor won't notice anything. You'll have to introduce Jacques as a friend of your painter" (for moneybags knew that his brother was being deceived, which he as an egoist found entertaining). "He loves being let into secrets, and we shall run less risk."

Osiris was prodigiously credulous. His mistress was fostering this security in letting him into the conspiracy against Lazare.

On one of the first nights when Nestor was lying asleep by her side, a young actor whom she liked rang her bell through having mistaken the date.

"Hide, it's my old man," she said to Osiris.

Osiris got up, collected his things, got into a wardrobe, was nearly suffocated in there while Germaine let the young man in, and went away bursting with pride.

Their relationship dated from this stroke of genius. Do not draw the conclusion that Germaine was dishonest. She was protecting herself. Her action was not calculated.

*   *   *

When they were very young her sister and she had dreamt of the Palais de Glace which they imagined as a hall of mirrors. Then went in one Sunday and came out followed by a train of handsome men. One of them seduced Germaine.

When he left her, she took a job with a milliner in Montmartre. The milliner said one day, "I am going to be arrested the day after tomorrow, my dear. Look after the shop, I'm clearing out." She took her pearls and her clothes.

Germaine stayed, put a card in the window announcing that four shilling hats were to be sold at sixpence, sold out in a morning, replaced the window display with soiled hats she found in the cellar, hired a cart with the money, moved the chairs, table and cheval glass out of the shop to the room which still belonged to her and let the bailiff take the rest.

She had the demon of the streets. She was not at all ashamed of it.

While dining with Loute, Nestor and Lazare in a

fashionable restaurant, she had knocked her wine over. The head waiter sprang forward and spread a piece of oilcloth over the stain until a table-cloth arrived. This piece of oilcloth reminded both sisters of one and the same thing. They glanced at each other. Loute blushed, but Germaine cried:

"Oh! that oilcloth. It takes me back to Belleville, the lamp, the soup, and father."

Their real name was Rateau. Since Nestor, the Rateaux were not to be pitied. They were the owners of a delightful farm near Paris.

*   *   *

The sisters, the Rateau farm, the Osirises, Jacques, his family and his dream make an explosive mixture. Yet it is shaped by fate, fond of handling men like chemicals.

*   *   *

If Jacques' multitudinous desires were to crystallise, and we were to approach them in the same way as we approach Germaine, would the result be any the more fit to tell?

Narcissus was in love with himself. For this crime the gods turned him into a flower. The flower gives us headaches and its onion-like bulb does not even

Their real name was Rateau.

make us cry. Would he deserve any more tears?

The story of our Narcissus is more complex. He was in love with the river. But rivers flow on heedless of the bathers, the trees they reflect. Their desire is the sea. At the end of a perpetual journey they kiss her and plunge voluptuously into her waters.

Jacques always felt that human beauty, like rivers, had a bed and a goal. It moved on, it went elsewhere. A ship weighs anchor, a curtain falls in the music-hall, the Ybreo family returns to its gods.

He recalled Idgi saying to him during a tennis match that he looked like Seti I. This was the only time he remembered the river looking at him.

This time the water stopped, ardently showing him his reflection. He deceived the sea. Perhaps he thought the water-sprite's voice was the water talking. But he did not analyse. His heart no longer gave him the time.

*　　　*　　　*

We have said that frequent demands were made on Germaine's heart. This habit did not lessen the enthusiasm she put into her escapades. She was in love every time for the first time. She wondered how she could ever have loved other men and played her new game showing all her cards. She did not try to make

57

the fire last by banking it up with cinders. She flared
up as high and as quickly as possible.

Her ability to put herself into a primitive state with
sincerity prevented her from meeting Jacques' passion
with the mechanical passion of a thoroughly exper-
ienced woman.

The storm threw their possessions together, regardless of their source.

For if Jacques had wasted a lot but brought his
dreams, Germaine who had given much, had received
much. And so she did not meet him empty-handed.

The last sentence lends itself to a double meaning.
There too Jacques' passion was stronger than his
scruples. Money-bags would be a husband, a deceived
husband.

Deceiving Nestor seemed so legitimate to Germaine
that she did not feel a shadow of uneasiness. The fail-
ure to realise things is contagious. The trick of pretending to be a friend of the painter seemed natural
to Jacques.

The dinner at which they met amused him. During
the dessert Germaine unthinkingly addressed him as
darling. He was on her right.

"Darling, did you read X's article . . . ?"

"You might reply, darling," she added almost without a break turning to the left to a Nestor stunned by

this stupendous three card trick. Afterwards they laughed at the warning.

Osiris took a liking to Jacques. He found he had a feeling for figures. Such an absurd opinion was due to the fact that Jacques listened to him. People either listened to him or they did not. He saw only this crude difference between men, not having the turn of mind which shows us the originality of each one.

The place where the young people really met was in the rue Daubigny, on a ground floor as dark as that painter's canvases.

The chambers belonged to Germaine. She argued that she needed a place to escape to when Nestor was visiting her. According to her explanation, she was going to find this place most convenient for the first time. She believed it. She was afraid of the caretaker Mme Supplice. And not in case the caretaker would think "another one," but in case she would be shocked to see that she no longer went in alone.

*   *   *

There is a limit to caresses, even the deepest. To all intents and purposes a virgin, Jacques was trying to satisfy a boundless desire. The first embrace disappointed him. In the course of time, as his dizziness subsided, he regained his quickness of sight and mind.

59

Then, when he studied this Desdemona lying back lifeless against the pillow, terrifyingly pale, her teeth bared, her face filled him with a host of shameful memories and he drew himself away from her like a knife.

Germaine distributed her full-blown caresses quickly. They were as extravagant as a florist's bouquet. When one bouquet fades, you buy another. But Jacques was taking root. His abnormal love was growing normally, slowly. He loved himself, he loved travel, he loved too many things in his mistress. Germaine loved only her lover.

Jea Cocteau
x 1957

Germaine's heart was often stirred.

V

This existence necessitated tricks in the rue de l'Estrapade, where Jacques idled away the hours that Germaine and Osiris spent together.

For the afternoons, he invented some work in the Sairte-Geneviève Library.

This library is the alibi of the young rascals in the Latin Quarter. If everyone who was supposed to be going there actually went, they would have to build a new wing. Jacques, who was friends again with Mouheddin and Louise, slept out one night in four. The Arab and he left the side-door half open. They shut it at dawn when they returned from their mistresses.

Louise saw Mouheddin in her room. The two accomplices met at the gates of the Park Monceau, and waited for the first Métro.

There was nothing funny in the way they left,

guillotined. They sat half asleep among the factory girls who were going to work.

*   *   *

It needed no great cunning to trick Berlin. He saw nothing and did not want to see anything. He asked no more than that his pupils and his salary should arrive on time.

His wife did use her eyes. They misled her. She was convinced that Jacques, smitten with love for her, incapable of deceiving his master, was fleeing her presence and drowning his sorrow with the girls at the Café Soufflet. She recommended the Arab to keep an eye on him.

*   *   *

Every Sunday, Stopwell found a mysterious incentive to win the jumping contest. During the week he was a rag, watching anxiously for the postman who was always supposed to be bringing him a cheque, living in the cloud rising from his pipe and tea-pot. His great body was splayed out all over the room. After dinner, he put on a silk suit and fell into a heavy sleep intoxicated with tobacco.

Petitcopain waited on this despot with the same expression as the girls who look after lunatics in hospitals. He divided his time between this job and the duty of look-out which he did for Mouheddin.

He had no grudge against Peter. Beneath his pose he discovered a host of weaknesses of a nature which he did not understand, but from which he inferred that he was vulnerable.

With the smell of Virginia tobacco he breathed in the poetry of England.

He loved Stopwell in the same way as the Latin races slowly succumb to London, the town with healthy red cheeks and a heart of black coal, a sleeping poppy.

In him he loved sleepiness, a royal chessboard, does on the grass, dukes marrying actresses, Chinese beside the Thames.

Stopwell's infrequent remarks were in praise of Oxford, paradise of colleges and little shops, with the best hellenists and the finest gloves in the world.

Through sitting hopefully by an attic window, like a princess in her tower, young Maricelles had fallen ill.

He was curing himself at the Chateau de Maricelles, near Maricelles-les-Maricelles, an address which was enough to amuse the boarders and provide a topic of conversation at dinner.

*　　　*　　　*

One Wednesday in November when Germaine and
Jacques were to meet Bashtarzi in Louise's room, they
saw a small thin woman in the sitting room, hatless,
and wearing an emerald pendant. It was her mother.
Jacques was astonished to recognise Mme Supplice,
the caretaker in the rue Daubigny. The house belonged to one of Louise's ex-protectors. Germaine had
never said anything about it.

"Good afternoon," said Germaine. "What a dress
you're wearing! Is Louise in?"

"No," replied the caretaker in a monotonous voice,
"the young lady has not come in yet."

They sat down. They coughed. But Mme Supplice
quickly grew more friendly. She launched into the
praises of Mouheddin, whom she believed to be a
Turkish Prince.

In any case Mouheddin was quite shy with intelli-
gent people and hid his stories from them, lost all
control with tradesmen and stupid people. You could
see that Mme Supplice's sentences, reeled straight off
without full stops or commas, were the stories that he
had to tell her since he could not shine in more
distinguished company.

Jacques did not dare look at Germaine. He would
have been very surprised to see that she was not
laughing. She smiled. She stood up.

"Good old mother, always the same!" she exclaimed and gave her a familiar pat on the knee.

Louise and Mouheddin came back. They seemed annoyed about the meeting, particularly Mouheddin.

*　　　*　　　*

Can a writer slip a story into the middle of his book when that story is superfluous to it? Yes, if the story brings out a character. Now it is important to bring out the fact that Louise was a good girl, but a good Supplice-Champagne girl.

Before our book begins, Louise used to dance at the Eldorado. Four schoolboys always went to applaud and throw her bouquets of violets. On the first of January they wanted to give her a pendant. The pickpocket of the group pinched an emerald from an old relative. He naïvely agreed that they should draw lots to decide who should present it. The lot fell on the shyest boy. Louise thanked him with a caress. They told themselves that to an actress an emerald is a drop of water in the ocean. They forgot that the ocean exists on drops of water.

A long time after the closing episode in this book the shy one, now a diplomat, met Louise. They revived old memories.

"You know the false emerald?" she said. "I gave it

to my mother. She always wore it. She wanted it to be buried with her."

The diplomat confessed that the emerald was stolen, and that it was real. Louise paled.

"Will you swear it?" she asked. And he dared not swear because Louise had just assumed the expression of a gravedigger.

*   *   *

Let us return to the rue Montchanin.

The two couples often used to go to a skating rink. They went there now. They knew the instructors and the barman.

A young man with a face like a washerwoman, wearing a cape and a pearl necklace was walking around the tables, smiling at some, bumping into others, shouting that spinning round had made him sick. His cultivated voice was like the ridiculous curves of the modern style.

This monster would have got himself hanged anywhere. There, he was a fetish. They fawned on him, they were honoured if he spoke to them. He shook hands with Germaine and Louise and simpered coquettishly at the men.

Jacques' dark side vainly sent a feeling of moral uneasiness to his light side. He had adopted a limp-

ing rythm. He liked it. He was walking along the roof-
tops without feeling giddy, like a sleepwalker.

The monster allowed them to sit down for a
minute. In a voice which was now quite faint he was
guessing the value of Louise's rings. He was showing
his own. He was telling stories about police raids.

When everything is moving at once, nothing appears
to be moving.

For Jacques to realise his spiritual laziness, there
would have had to be a fixed point. That he should
have imagined his father or mother walking across
the promenade, for example.

But his actions were far from them, far from himself. He was lying happily in the dirty water.

He would have felt disgusted had he been alone in
such a place. As he was blended with Germaine who
talked to the fetish on equal terms, he did not rebel,
and had an easy time.

The orchestra was playing a fashionable dance.

Fashions die young. That is what makes their gaiety
so grave. The dance was swollen with the assurance of
success and with melancholy because it would soon be
forgotten. One day every note of it would pierce
Jacques' heart. They skated.

During a pause in which the monster performed a
number, Louise gave a little scream: "You!" And,

looking away from the rink, they all saw a jovial Osiris leaning on his stick, with the electric light bulbs reflecting on his nose, his top hat, his pearl tie-pin.

"Yes children, me, me. And quite satisfied too. For several days I have been assailed with anonymous letters saying that Germaine spends all her time at the skating rink with a lover. I wanted to verify it and I consider it to be untrue. And that's it," he concluded, laying his hand on Jacques' shoulder, "for between you and me, my friend, I don't want to say anything nasty (tastes differ) but you are not her type."

He sat down. Germaine beat him with her fists, spoke threateningly to him, and put on a straight face.

"In any case," he said opening a card-case, "I think I recognize Lazare's writing. Perhaps this is his revenge. Here, Jacques my boy, take these letters, study them. You young people are being brought up on traveller's tales. You can make a better guess than an old fool like me."

"Do we love our old fool?" he lisped, tickling Germaine under the chin, "do we love him?"

And Germaine, now securely mounted in the saddle again, replied, "No, we don't love him. We don't love sneaks."

*   *   *

Madeleine aine joli yeux louchons
Ses doigts avec ma main trichaient dans le manchon
Elle m'a fait du mal autant qu'a su faire

(opize)

Jean
*

Germaine, with her pretty, squinting eyes, fingered my hands, playing tricks in the muff. She did me as much harm as could have been done.

Jacques' life was like the rooms of Montmartre women that are never cleaned because they get up at four o'clock and slip a coat over their nightgown to go downstairs and eat.

This state of affairs always gets worse. Nestor stopped showing letters, stopped laughing. He did not suspect Jacques, in spite of precise accusations; he suspected Germaine. Blinded by conceit, he would gladly have admitted that she might deceive him with a man as stout and as old as he, what he ingenuously called his type, but that it might be with little Jacques would have been too much for him to believe. He did not hesitate a moment. He confided in him and asked him to keep an eye on Germaine.

"I have to live at the Bourse and I often work at night. Follow her. Do not leave her. Do be so kind."

Now, Nestor Osiris began to make scenes. He had not started threatening yet, he broke ornaments. Germaine had noticed that he gave her a Copenhagen ornament every time they made it up. In this way he could break things without doing much damage. He avoided Chinese vases and earthenware.

When he broke a Dresden china group, Germaine knew that the vaudeville had turned to tragedy. He broke open cupboards, hunted for fingerprints, bribed manicurists, lost his head.

73

Returning from the dentist one evening he found Germaine on the chaise longue. He asked her if she had had company. She replied that she had not, that she had been sleeping and reading since lunch. It was true.

Nestor went out to hang his fur coat in the cloakroom. He reappeared brandishing a cane with a tortoiseshell top.

"And what's this? What's this?" he shouted. "Since your gentleman friend leaves his canes in my room, I'll use this to teach you a lesson."

Germaine closed the book.

"You're crazy," she said. "Get out."

The telephone rang.

"Don't touch the receiver," shouted Nestor. "If it's the man with the cane, I'm the one who will speak to him."

In fact, it was about the cane. The dentist asked Mr. Osiris if there had not been a mistake, as his patient had found one with the initials N.O. instead of his own, which had a tortoise-shell top.

Germaine enjoyed the modest triumph. The episode gave her four days peace.

*   *   *

The Osiris brothers went shooting on Sundays.

They left at five o'clock on the previous evening. So Germaine was free. This Saturday, Nestor stayed, sacrificing the shooting. It was a chivalrous way of making her forgive him.

Germaine hid her disappointment. She warned Jacques. He was to be sensible and stay in the rue de l'Estrapade, and go to bed early.

At nine o'clock, Jacques was reading in his room like the other boys (except Mouheddin) when they heard a timid ring at the bell on their floor.

After answering the bell and whispering, Petitcopain, who acted as caretaker, knocked on Jacques' door. He announced a visitor. It was Germaine. She was carrying a bag. Jacques couldn't get over it.

Some reflex made him kick an old pair of socks under the chest of drawers. Germaine teased him for being so dazed.

She was bored with Nestor at dinner-time. She had said, "Wait for me; I am going to make a salad in the kitchen for a surprise." She had taken clothes, toilet things and had escaped down the service stairs.

"Don't scold me, my love," she begged. "I am free, free, free. Let him break everything. I am taking you on a honeymoon trip."

*　　　　*　　　　*

A road can sometimes look so different on the way out and on the way back that the traveller, coming home, thinks he is lost.

The village where one lives, seen suddenly from a hill, can be mistaken for another village.

Because of Germaine's presence in the rue de l'Estrapade, Jacques hardly recognised his mistress, and no longer recognised his room.

It took him a minute to admit the proposition, namely: to go away by train and spend Sunday on the farm that belonged to the Rateaux who had gone to le Havre.

After the initial shock, Jacques was as madly enthusiastic as she. They christened the trip *Round the World*. Jacques would have to go down and see the master's wife, tell her that he was going out and would not be back until Monday morning, to work.

Not wanting to leave Germaine in his room, as Peter might have gone in, he shut her in Maricelles' empty room with a lamp and cigarettes. She was in no danger there.

On the floor below, Jacques found the master and his wife in the process of setting the clock. They had to wait for it to strike all the hours and half-hours. Then Jacques, who usually went out every Saturday night, announced that he was going to spend Sunday in the country at a friend's house.

The Berlins gave their permission, on the condition that the boy reported to his master's study on Monday morning. Jacques went upstairs, released Germaine, and they got their things ready.

Everything went into one bag. This delighted them. They smothered their hysterical laughter. Still playing at *Round The World*, Jacques said in a whisper that they would have to be careful on the crossing outside the cabin that belonged to a fierce Englishman, with a red moustache, a bag of bank notes, and a veil made out of a butterfly net. He had been on their track since Liverpool and was plotting their downfall.

They went downstairs without any difficulty, using a box of matches, and found the cab that Germaine had left at the corner of the rue Mouffetard.

VI

To describe the journey I would need all the delightful apparatus of a conjurer. Flags, bouquets, lanterns, eggs, and goldfish.

Miraculously, Germaine still had the down of her girlhood. It had often been plucked. Jacques had a protection against the mud like the grease which prevents water from making swans wet. But both of them passed the first snow-laden trees, the first animal, like a sleepwalker passing the refuse carts in les Halles on his way home at five o'clock in the morning.

But this was unimportant. The country was part of Germaine's heritage. She was returning to a lost paradise, and Jacques was Jacques no longer, but Germaine, that is to say one of the high carts so fresh at dawn in the place de la Concorde where the market gardeners lie asleep, cradled like the idle kings on their litters of cabbages and roses.

Germaine really was misleading him. The conjurer could almost have been the Spring in person, using his boxes with false bottoms.

How could this early harvest, false as it was, seem anything but real to Jacques who had borne with the fetish at the skating rink?

Thousands of roads lead away from the white, one leads towards it, says Montaigne. Jacques went for the white. He held Germaine close, kept her warm in the carriage and let himself behave like a child.

Jacques disliked himself, but he was not disliked. Germaine and he made an attractive couple. They were taken for two innocent lovers on an excursion.

What spontaneity, what surprises! But the only place where the poor girl had any surprises left was up her sleeve.

Jacques could not see the strings any more than the children who clap. It is a good start to be able to make children clap.

Germaine, whose old tricks were well-practised, sincerely believed that she was gathering watches and doves. The illusionist shared in the illusions of the public.

So this trip was the only ethereal happiness they had.

The farm was small. Germaine was on familiar

terms with the servants and the cows. She walked about with a pack of young dogs snapping playfully at her heels. She shouted, jumped about, took her hair down.

They lunched in a room where the fire was a great blaze. They ate the clean food that one cannot eat in town. The cheese, knowledgeably ripened in a vine leaf was the only thing that contrasted vividly with the meat and the white cream.

After lunch, Germaine showed him the room that belonged to her father, an old drunkard. It was impossible to cure him of his vice.

In the middle of the room hung a multi-coloured paper chandelier. On the chest of drawers stood pale photographs of sailors, weddings, and, under a piece of glass, half a frigate stuck on to painted green waves.

"Here I am as a virgin," said Germaine, holding a frame of sea-shells in front of Jacques. It surrounded a naked baby.

She had her own room. They went to bed there and adored each other for the last time. Did Jacques foresee it? Not in the slightest. Neither did Germaine. They were right, as they were often to make love afterwards.

*   *   *

They left at dawn two days later, not at all tired. They could hear the cocks taking up the infectious cry one after the other like the burners of a huge chandelier lighting up. Everything was frozen, wet, virginal. Germaine went about jauntily with a red nose. She had not a single wrinkle to disturb the pure morning.

She had discovered an old photograph in her chest of drawers. She was screwing up her eyes as if she were short-sighted. Jacques thought this face was divine. Germaine gave it to him.

Besides that they brought back eggs and cheese. They really did go round the world.

*   *   *

In that short time Germaine had forgotten what the streets of Paris looked like. This surprise prolonged the escapade. She was getting back to her normal life again without feeling sorry. The cries of the trades-men, the lean runners training behind the cyclists, the maids beating carpets out of the windows, the steaming horses, reminded her of her childhood.

They decided that after his work Jacques should have lunch at Germaine's flat. They took a taxi, for she wanted to go back with him.

The chauffeur drove like a madman, skidded,

mounted the islands. Germaine and Jacques enjoyed themselves, kissed on the mouth, bumped their teeth, were thrown all over each other. At each new feat, the driver turned round, shrugged his shoulders, and winked at them.

Germaine dropped Jacques in the rue de l'Estrapade about ten o'clock, after a long embrace. He went on watching her waving her glove as the car went on its way. He arrived like Phileas Fogg, just in time to change and appear at the right moment with his fellow students in the study, where M. Berlin was trying to teach Geography.

*   *   *

Germaine went into a Post Office and telephoned her flat. Josephine, who had been told on the famous evening to say to Osiris that she had not seen Madame go out, described the poor man's fury, the way he searched, begged, and cursed. He had broken a mirror and cried, being superstitious. He had spent Sunday anxiously walking up and down, watching the telephone and the cars. Finally, on Sunday night, he said quietly, "Josephine, whether Madame comes back or not, I am leaving her. You can tell her that from me. Sort my things out. I am leaving the rest for her. Let her do whatever she likes with it."

"Phew!" sighed Germaine. "Good luck."

She knew that a beautiful girl is never in difficulties for long.

On her way in she met her sister.

"Didn't I tell you often enough what would happen?" cried Loute. "Nestor won't see you again. When people talk about you, he spits."

"Let him spit," replied Germaine.

"I'm suffocated. I have just come back from the country with Jacques. Nestor is stuffy."

"How will you live?"

"Don't worry, little Loute. Besides, Nestor is a fly-paper; he sticks. I should be very surprised if he didn't try to come back."

Osiris came back so quickly that he passed Loute on her way out. Germaine, who had gone to bed, kept him waiting.

When he came in, he stopped, bowed, and went to sit down on a chair at the foot of the bed.

"My dear Germaine," he began.

"Is this a speech?"

He struck an attitude.

"My dear Germaine . . . everything is over between us, ov-er. I have written you a final letter, but as I know how careless you are and the way you read letters, I have come to read it to you."

83

"Do you realise that you are being ridiculous beyond bounds?"

"That is possible," continued Nestor, "but you must hear my letter."

He took it out of his pocket.

"I won't hear it."

"You will."

"No."

"Yes."

"No."

"Very well. I shall read it all the same."

She put her fingers in her ear and hummed. In the voice of one used to calling the prices at the Bourse, Osiris began.

"My poor little lunatic . . ."

Germaine burst out laughing.

"The lady laughs, the lady is listening," remarked Nestor. "So I shall continue."

But this time Germaine hummed her loudest and it was impossible for him to read. Nestor put the letter down on his knee.

"Very well, I'll stop," he said.

She took her fingers out of her ears.

"Only I warn you" (he shook his first finger admonishingly, "that if you don't let me read it, I shall leave. And you will ne-ver see me again."

Germaine to Nestor:
I have nothing to account for.

"Because it is your final letter."

"There are ends and ends," stammered Osiris, who had a gift for ciphers; that is to say, for poetry, and who was absolutely stupid in love where such poetry does not exist.

"——I wanted to end it in a nice way, in a proper way, and you are hounding me out. Supposing I called you to account!"

"I have nothing to account for," burst out Germaine, who was exasperated by this play-acting, "and if you want an account, here it is: yes, I am deceiving you. I have a lover. Yes, I sleep with Jacques." And with every yes she tugged at her plait as if it were a bell pull.

"My word!" said Osiris, standing up, stepping back and screwing up his eyes like a painter. He accused Germaine of pinning the suspicion on an obliging boy, hoping that he, Osiris, would rush off to find him while she entertained her real lover.

He added that he was not taken in; that he might be the rich man being taken for a ride, but being rich was a profession; an exacting profession that makes one observant.

*   *   *

Germaine was full of admiration. Despite the plays

she had seen, she had not believed that anyone like this existed.

"You are superb, Nestor," she said. "I sleep with Jacques. In any case" (the bell rang) "this is sure to be him. He is coming to lunch. Hide, and you will see the proof for yourself."

She wanted to end it.

"Hide," said Osiris with a derisive laugh. "That is too easy. You have plenty of tricks in your bag, and you will signal. I am staying."

And as they heard a door opening, and Jacques' voice off-stage, he shouted:

"My dear Jacques, do you know what Germaine has thought up?"

Jacques came in.

"You sleep with her!"

*   *   *

From his contact with Germaine, Jacques had learnt her tricks. He understood the scene at a glance, and saw that his mistress, tired to death, had given everything away.

"Let us keep calm, Monsieur Osiris," he said. "You know that Germaine likes teasing. She teases you because she loves you."

The pure-hearted Jacques did so well that Nestor

stayed to lunch and opened a box of cigars.

Queens of Egypt! The contents of that richly painted box were like your tiny mummies with their golden girdles.

Osiris ate, smoked, laughed and left for the Bourse.

Germaine sulked and reproached Jacques for his cunning.

"Then you don't want to be the only one?"

"I don't want to be responsible for such a serious thing and for you to blame me for it one day."

The farm, the milk, the eggs, were far away.

* * *

When Lazare questioned his brother, Nestor gave him a pat on the shoulder.

"Germaine is a character," he said. "That is her charm. We shan't change her. She was at her farm. She needed cows. We men of the Bourse don't understand it. Loute is simple, what shall I say—less lively, less colourful. Again, she has her points. I am keeping Germaine."

This episode appeared to restore Osiris to his former position. Insinuations, anonymous letters made him smile in a superior way as if he knew a secret which might mean that Germaine laid herself open to scandal-mongers, but which was to the advantage of her rich lover. This vague secret had something to do with his mistress' superiority, her love of nature, and her rearing dogs.

If he was asked "Where is Germaine?" he would reply, "I give her a great deal of freedom. I don't interfere."

Loute was amazed. As she herself lacked an easy manner and talents, she considered her sister very strong.

VII

Like dirty clothes, boxes, and combs lying about an hotel room, the affair was dragging on. Jacques had no reason to suffer from this disorder. He no longer saw it. He saw only through the eyes of his mistress, who had been accustomed to live in this way since her childhood. A new element came to swell the disorder.

For three weeks Germaine had been having bad news of her father. She did not like him and burnt the letters.

"It's our business to go out at night, you know," Louise would say.

But Germaine, who thought herself more 'respectable' rather looked down on Louise, and imagined that shutting her eyes to her father's condition would leave her more freedom. She even pretended to think that her mother was exaggerating, flying into a panic for nothing.

One evening when she was dressing to go to a revue with Jacques and Osiris, Jacques found a telegram half-hidden beneath the telephone: *Urgent father dying come love.* She hid it so that she could go to the theatre. Jacques showed it to her in silence.

"Leave it alone," she said, as she put on her lipstick, pressing her lips together afterwards, "I'll go tomorrow."

During the interval Rateau passed away on his farm at eleven o'clock.

For two weeks Mme Rateau had been reading him *La Maison du Baigneur*, in which Siete-Iglesias is crushed by a mechanical ceiling. Rateau confused this chapter with reality. He thought he was Iglesias and died lying on the floor, his face turned to one side, trying to take up as little space as possible, crushed by the ceiling of his room, in front of his horrified wife.

*　　　　*　　　　*

M. Rateau left to his wife all he had had from his daughter, and insisted on being buried in the family vault at Père-Lachaise. Osiris ordered a motor hearse.

Loute had quarrelled with her mother.

As Germaine refused to go alone to the farm to fetch the body, Jacques asked for special leave from the

Rue de l'Estrapade. Nestor lent his car which would hold the road better than the limousine. The hearse left half a day in advance.

This trip to the farm was not as delightful as the other. The driver had a little mirror so that he could see behind. It was important for them to be on their guard.

Germaine organised the return. She liked her mother. She would put her up for a fortnight in Paris. She took three rooms below her flat which were used for storing furniture. Orders were given for some of the furniture to be taken down to the linen room, and for the three rooms to be furnished with the rest. Mme Rateau would have a little home of her own.

Her daughter made plans and grew sentimental.

Incapable of pretence, except with Nestor, she did not shed a single tear over the drunken father who had beaten her too often. In her eyes her mother was freed.

*   *   *

Mme Rateau came to meet them. She was weeping, holding a handkerchief in one hand, and a Spanish fan in the other.

Since she had stopped working she had let her nails

93

grow and not knowing where to put her hands, she was never parted from the fan.

Her figure looked like a Lotto bag. She had regular commonplace features, a blotchy skin, and a white wig which emphasised her complexion—that of an English judge.

Her daughter introduced Jacques. The widow looked at him like a person suffering from seasickness.

The coffin was in the room where the young people had lunched on their trip *Round the World.*

Germaine managed to play the part tactfully. She decided that Mme Rateau should go in the car and the hearse should follow.

Every time the hearse was mentioned, Mme Rateau shook her head and repeated,

"A motor hearse . . . a motor hearse."

The return journey was pitiful. Germaine tapped on the windows. She was restraining the driver so that M. Rateau could follow.

Suddenly she turned round, looked through the window and exclaimed,

"Where is it?"

The road stretched away into the distance with no hearse.

They halted and turned back to look for the body. They found it. It was in a side street with a puncture.

The wheel would have to be changed. The jack was not working properly. Jacques and the driver set to work.

After an hour's struggle, with Mme Rateau shaking her head in encouragement, worn out with hiccoughs and tears, they set off again.

As luck would have it, Jacques' silence irritated Germaine and she dropped him in the rue de l'Estrapade, so that for one moment the drivers could imagine that they were conducting the body of a famous man to the Pantheon.

*   *   *

Mme Rateau's mourning dress kept the fashionable dressmakers and milliners busy. Feeling it to be respectable to have a widowed mother, Germaine put her on show. She took her to her shops. Mme Rateau appreciated this luxury. She picked up bits of crêpe everywhere. She had crêpe dresses, dressing gowns, tippets, toques, cloaks, and hoods. What is more, she took care of her mourning dress, and never went out if there was a chance of rain. *"Crêpe is like sunshine for lunch,"* she said.

No one hesitates to lay a wreath of brightly-coloured flowers on a tomb, and Mme Rateau did not give up her fan.

One Sunday when Germaine was taking her to Versailles, inflicting this duty on Jacques, the silence which reigned in the car as far as the Bois de Boulogne gave him the opportunity of studying the fan.

It depicted the death of Gallito.

*　　　　　*　　　　　*

Nothing is more like a sunset than a corrida. Gracefully lowering its powerful neck, its Antinuos' brow, wide and curly, the bull was watching the crowd and goring the fallen matador in the stomach with its right horn. In the middle distance, to the left, a picador on a bloody horse whose ribs could be counted like the Spanish Christ was trying to prick the simple beast which was shaking the bunch of bandilleros on its neck.

A man was scaling the outer wall on the extreme left, and like the Aeginian archer who is said to be on his knees shooting to fill up a corner, a humpbacked ring-hand filled up the extreme right with his hump.

*　　　　　*　　　　　*

Jacques was growing bored. The crêpe intimidated him. He did not dare take Germaine's knees between his legs.

"Gallito," he kept saying stupidly, "Gallito, Gal, gal, gal." And the gal reminded him of Victor Hugo's lines:

Gall, amant de la reine, alla, tour magnanime
Galamment, de l'arène a la Tour Magne, à Nîme.

So he recited them under his breath as if he were humming.

"What are you reciting?" asked Germaine.

"Nothing. I remembered two lines by Victor Hugo."

"Say them again."

"Gall, amant de la reine, alla, tour magnanime
Galamment, de l'arène à la Tour Magne, à Nîme."

"What does that mean?"

"Gall: a M. Gall who was the queen's lover; went on a magnanimous journey: chivalrously—from the arena, as on your mother's fan: to a tower called Magne: at Nîmes, the town."

"Animates the town?"

"No. Nîmes, Nîmes, Nîmes the town.'

"So what?"

"So nothing."

"Victor Hugo was trying to make fools of everyone the day he wrote those lines."

"But it's deliberate, it's a joke."

"I don't think it's funny."

"It wasn't meant to be funny."

"Now I really don't understand."

"They are two lines that sound the same and look different."

"Explain."

"Instead of rhyming at the end, these two lines rhyme the whole way through."

"Then they aren't rhymes, if they are the same."

"But they aren't the same because they say something different. It's a triumph of wit."

"I don't see how it's a triumph of wit. I'd have dozens of triumphs of wit if all I had to do was to repeat the same thing twice running and call it lines of poetry."

"Look, little Germaine, listen; you aren't listening."

"Thank you. Treat me like a fool."

"Oh! Germaine."

"Don't let's talk about it any more, if I am incapable of understanding."

"I never said you were incapable of understanding. You ask me to explain the lines. I explain, and you get angry . . ."

"I get angry, do I Well! I don't care two hoots for your Victor Hugo."

"To start with, Victor Hugo is not mine Secondly, I love you. Those lines are silly. Don't let's talk about them any more."

Germaine advised Jacques to do
more work for his examinations.

"You didn't think they were silly a minute ago. Now you think they are silly so that I'll leave you alone."

"We have never argued. Are we going to do so for such a ridiculous reason?"

"Just as you like. I ask you nicely, and because you are thinking about something else and I am disturbing you, you give me a lump of sugar."

"This is not like you."

"Nor you."

*　　　　*　　　　*

This vulgar scene, the first between Germaine and Jacques, had been going on since the Bois de Boulogne. After her *nor you* Germaine turned away and looked at the trees. Mme Rateau went on fanning herself.

They reached Versailles and had tea at the Hôtel des Reservoirs without Germaine or her mother speaking. On the way back Germaine broke the silence, and said in a submissive voice,

"Jacques my love, those lines . . ."

"Oh!"

"Will you teach them to me?"

"Listen. I'll give them to you in detail: Gall—

amant—de—la—reine—alla—tour—magnanime. Galamment—de—l'arène—à—la Tour Magne—à Nîme. '

"You see, it is the same thing."

"No it's not."

"You say it's not and you don't prove anything."

"There's nothing to prove. It's a famous example."

"It's famous?"

"Yes."

"Very famous."

"Yes."

"Then how can it be that I don't know it?"

"Because you are not interested in literature."

"That's what I said. I'm a fool."

"Listen, Germaine, you are the reverse of a fool,
but you are frightening me today. You are deliberately trying to frighten me."

"That's the last straw."

"How sad that we should hurt each other for such
an asinine thing."

"You're telling me!"

"That's enough. I don't feel well. I demand silence,
it's my turn.'

And so they went on until they were on the verge
of sticking pins in one another. Then Mme Rateau
came out of her dumb silence.

"You see, children," she said, folding up her fan,

"none of that prevented this Gall from being the queen's lover."

These words from a mother disclosed a perfect grasp of the facts.

Mme Rateau spoke little, but well. It was either "my poor husband was carried away in one hour" or "what? Paris was called Lutetia, M. Jacques? That's news."

As she was enthusing over "a superb statue of Henri IV," Jacques mechanically asked her if it was an equestrian one. She hesitated, only to reply "so-so" spontaneously defining the centaur.

Germaine held her sides. Mme Rateau was annoyed. Jacques was completely at sea.

*   *   *

The day after the Gall business, he woke up feeling unhappy.

Just as a patient after an operation thinks of cold drinks, a man with an injured spine, being unable to sit down, draws chairs, he dreamt of the discreet wives who help their men in their work, and found a family. But he thrust this thirst for cold water away as if it were a thirst for alcohol.

*   *   *

One night when he was holding Germaine tight, he whispered that he would like a child. Germaine confessed that this pleasure was denied to her.

"I should already have had one if it were possible," she said. "I make up for it by rearing fox terriers."

The peach reveals its worm. Most of them conceal one. Poor Jacques; it would have been very rash for him to have changed his lot for that of the king's beasts, as he longed to do. On assuming their form, surely one would feel some deep-seated infirmity apart from the flaws which cannot be seen through park trees or bar smoke.

These successive blows in no way estranged him from Germaine. On the contrary. He pitied her. So he pitied himself. His love grew, and slept like a baby rocked in its cradle.

*   *   *

There was a surprise party at Germaine's. The Castor Sugar crowd came to tea unexpectedly.

Castor Sugar was sixty and looked twenty-five. Her diet consisted in drinking nothing but champagne and never sleeping, except with jockeys and dancing teachers. She kept an opium den. There were Japanese robes of crêpe de chine to wear. Everyone lay smoking in a tangled heap on a rug. They listened to the late Caruso singing *Pagliacci*.

This delightful company shouted, jumped and boxed.

About seven o'clock they all crammed into a Black Maria with a white chauffeur, blind deaf and dumb like a statue of cocaine.

When Jacques and Germaine went up to Mme Rateau's room they could see her sitting down with her back to them. Her fan alone was moving.

"Hello, mother."

"Hello, Germaine."

"You sound queer."

"No . . . no."

"Yes you do."

"No I don't."

"Yes you do, Mme Rateau, you do sound queer. Jacques can tell that there is something wrong with you."

"Well, since you force me to it," said the widow, "I admit that I find it strange that people should give parties without asking me to come down."

"But look here mother, your mind is on other things. To start with, you are in mourning" (her daughter forgot that she was in mourning too) "and then I really can't take you to meet Mlle Sugar."

*   *   *

This extraordinary excuse opened a secret door to Jacques. A woman can look at a magazine cover and see the same woman looking at the same magazine and so on until the point where the picture stops for lack of space, but it continues as before when we think we have come to the bottom of one class of society. There are still millions capable of saying with a certain king: "I am farther from my sister than my sister is from her chief gardener."

Jacques accepted all that. He was too much part of his mistress to judge her actions or her family. Now his dark side was sprinkling clouds of ink over his light side like a cuttle-fish. After helping him, it was gently making him blind.

Louise offered herself to Mouheddin and Mouheddin to Louise. This loveless exchange exhilarated them. Parallel to the Jacques-Germaine drama they were having an indecently gay time.

Louise received cheques from a foreign prince. This prince was coming to the throne and rarely left his future kingdom. He came to London for the conferences where great men meet. Then he spent two weeks with Louise. He told her the secrets of Europe, and how the puerile kings, cooped up together, played practical jokes on each other and moved the shoes around outside the doors. He even wrote to her, and Mme Supplice often said in her "exceptionally lucid woman's" voice, "if ever His Highness leaves little Louise, she shall take his letters to the frontier. It amazes me that a prince should write such things. She shall take them. She has him."

In short, Louise lived in freedom except when there were big political upheavals.

On the fifteenth of every month, an officer with a blue moustache turned into the rue Montchanin, clicked his heels, and delivered an envelope.

Mouheddin admired his uniform through the lavatory ventilator.

One morning, about six o'clock, when Mouheddin was dressing to meet Jacques, he had the idea of a joke. Louise was asleep. On the bedside table there was a box full of loose change and rings. This joke, which was more or less funny, consisted in dropping one coin noisily on top of the others, and wakening the sleeper, as if they were a couple at a shady hotel.

Sleep has its own universe, geographies, geometries, calendars. It may take us back to the Ark. Then we rediscover a mysterious knowledge of the sea. We swim, and we seem to be flying with no effort.

Louise's memories did not go back so far. The

noise of the coin brought her back from a dream nearer the surface.

"Gustave," she sighed, "do leave me something for lunch."

Her sigh was ten years old.

This episode astonished Mouheddin. He laughed all alone in the empty street. Jacques was waiting for him. He told him what a coin can do when it falls into a sleeping marsh.

"Poor girl," said Jacques, "don't tell her anything about it."

"You dramatize everything," burst out Mouheddin. "You're wrong. You poison your own life."

In the métro, Jacques noticed that he had forgotten his wrist-watch. He did not see Germaine the next day. The day after that, he went to the rue Daubigny at ten o'clock to get it back.

Mme Supplice was not in the caretaker's room. He put the key in the lock, turned it, crossed the hall, opened the door. What did he see? Germaine and Louise.

*　　　　　*　　　　　*

They were asleep, intertwined like a monogram, in such an extraordinary way that the limbs of one seemed to belong to the other. Imagine the Queen of Hearts without her robe.

At the sight of these white forms spread out on the sheet, Jacques went as stupid as Perrette at the sight of her spilt milk. Should he kill? This would have been very ridiculous, and what is more, a pleonasm. It seemed impossible to make this dead couple any more dead. Except that Germaine's open mouth was moving, and Louise's legs were twitching like a sleeping dog's.

It was striking how natural the sight appeared.

You would have said that these candid positions brought out their beauty. Having always known vice, they found it a relaxation.

From what sea had this drowned couple risen? Doubteless they had come a long way. They had been tossed by all the waves and all the moons since Lesbos to be laid out there under a foam of lace and muslin.

*   *   *

Jacques felt so awkward that he thought of going out and leaving no traces. But, as Jesus revives a sinner, so his presence revived Louise.

"Is it you, mother?" she said with half-open eyes. She opened them and recognised Jacques.

He had to smile or fight. Jacques muttered:

"This is a fine thing."

"What, a fine thing?" cried Germaine. "Would you rather I deceived you with a man?"

If she is still in love, this kind of woman thinks of a lie. But without realising it, she was no longer in love. Since the Sunday at the farm, the light had gone out and her love was only a habit.

"You are young," Louise concluded, yawning.

Jacques took the wrist watch and ran out.

Once in the Berlin establishment he realised his stupidity. After a burst of individuality, he was again seeing things from Germaine's angle. He told his discovery to Mouheddin who knew about the relationship between the girls.

"You're working yourself up," he said. "Moral laws are the rules of a game at which everyone cheats, and has done so since the beginning of the world. We shan't change it. Go and meet them at the skating rink at four. I have a lesson. I'll come for you at six."

Jacques shaved, studied the short-sighted picture, congratulated himself on having an Osiris and a Louise as rivals, scribbled off a Greek translation, and ran to the skating rink. They were having a benefit gala for a musicians' charity fund.

VIII

The skating rink was crowded. The Vesuvian rumble of the skates on the concrete was deafening, even during the intervals. A negro band alternated with an organ. The negroes flung trumpet notes at one another like lumps of raw meat.

Near the organ, which was vomiting behind a flimsy staircase, a woman in mourning was writing letters at a little table. She changed the bands. A dismal crowd spun round, each thinking he was surrounded by empty space. On the lower floor there was a delightful slate shooting range decorated with pipes, red targets, a host of rabbits, palm trees, zouaves. The fountain with an egg bobbing on top was a tulip plant. A shot would cut the flower off. The woman in charge of the range leant over and put the flower back on again. Men in sweaters played bowls. Heard from above, between the two kinds of music, the bowls thudded

111

like shoe trees being thrown about a room.

On the balcony, from which there was a view of the whole hall, stood two American marines with profiles like Dante and Virgil, their ribbons whipped crazily by the ventilators as they leant over the gulf. The decorations were banners and floodlights.

One number consisted of a revival of the can-can. Eight women, survivors from the golden age, shook a real bird-cage to the rhythm of Offenbach. Sometimes nothing could be distinguished but their black legs in silks and satins from the Palais Royal; sometimes they threw their feet up in the air with their hands like champagne corks and were drowned in the froth below. There is no more foam in the Birth of Venus.

This dance rouses the Parisian as the corrida rouses the Spaniard. It finishes with the splits, a group on a transparent postcard on which the Eiffel Tower, old stager that she is, smiles, bursting her steel bodice, split open to the very heart.

*   *   *

In spite of the crush, Jacques found the two girls sitting down. The picture of them as a Hindu idol haunted him. He had to make an effort to see them apart.

"Here," said Germaine, "it's too cold; take my glass."

Jacques was drinking, happy to put a straw through which Germaine had drunk into his mouth, when a bump knocked down the fence surrounding the rink so that it hit the table. Two red hands grasped the plush balustrade. Jacques looked up. It was Stopwell.

"Hello Jacques! Excuse me, I was skating, and recognized you. I always fall like a thunderbolt. I didn't know you came to the rink."

"But if you come often," Jacques shouted, because of the organ which prevented him hearing himself, "why have I never seen you here before?"

"I went skating elsewhere. Tonight I'm here for the music."

He disappeared across the rink.

"Who is he?" asked Germaine.

"It's that Englishman, the dreadful Englishman in *Round the World*."

"Ask him to join us," said Louise, "he's alone; you never even asked him to sit at our table."

*   *   *

This is the way clouds group together, the air is freshened, plants lean over and the water takes on a pearly hue.

*　　　　*　　　　*

Jacques went to find Stopwell and Stopwell came and sat between Germaine and Louise.

As Verlaine said of Lucien Létinois: *"He skated marvellously."* He wore knickerbockers, charming English trousers which buckle below the knee and hang down over the leg, tartan stockings, a soft shirt, and a tie with his Club stripes. His easy grace impressed Jacques.

He always saw him as part of the Berlin set-up; and, like a canvas which makes a poor effect without a frame and lighting and only appears in its full power when it is finally framed against a wall in harsh lighting, so Stopwell took on new proportions at the skating rink.

Germaine was talking about masculine elegance Jacques, who was riled, was arguing that the elegance of Englishmen was regimented, that French elegance was superior by its very originality. He cited the dress of various members of the Jockey Club who had a charming originality which was all their own. He wanted to evoke the fiery silhouette of the duc de Montmorency, threadbare, stained, taking his opera hat to the dining-table.

114

He saw Peter and Germaine, monks by El Greco.

He missed his effect. Approaching disaster deprives a man of all his resources.

Stopwell upheld his speech. Stopwell spoke. He stressed his mistakes in French. This was the first time he had talked. At the Berlins' he did not condescend to do so. He was talking about England. He was a sailor talking about his ship. Jacques was right; Stopwell thought him noble. He leant out of his chair on the extreme right. His head was bowed.

Now Stopwell was crushing him with an indirect reply. He was speaking of elegance. He broke up his sentences with polite *you knows*, as terrible as his hand-shake.

"There is true elegance in London, you know," he said. "Opposite Rumpelmayer for example" (he was speaking to the women) . . . "Lock's little hat shop. It is a very dark, very small thing; so small that the assistants nail up the boxes in the street. All the coal of England" (and Stopwell assumed the voice of Lady Macbeth when she speaks the famous phrase "All the perfumes of Arabia . . .") "all the coal of England went to make this little diamond. Behind his window, as you say, you can see very, very old headgear, a century old, white with dust. M. Lock never brushes them. And when Lord Ribblesdale tries his hat on . . . then, you know . . . it's magnificent."

117

He scanned the magnificent and stressed the *mag* and *fic*, thrusting his hands into his trouser pockets, stuffed with chains and nickel keys.

The women were silent.

Germaine was drinking in his words. She was goggling at him. Jacques was desperate, for he saw the woman in whom he was incorporated separating herself from him without any transition, and himself diminishing as she went away. Like the cobbler in the *Arabian Nights* he was resuming his original shape. He was turning back into the man he was before their love affair.

The physical and mental agony was too much for him.

"What is the matter with you, my little Jacques?" asked Louise. "Your lips are trembling."

But Germaine heard neither the question nor the answer.

"Up!" commanded Stopwell, standing up on his skates, "come and skate with me."

Germaine left the table and followed him like a slave.

*   *   *

Jacques watched the rink. It was drawn out and bent in the distorting mirrors. The music was chang-

ing too, as it does when you play at putting your
fingers in your ears and taking them out again while
you listen to an orchestra. He saw Peter and Germaine, monks by El Greco. They were lengthened,
they turned green, they rose skywards in a swoon,
caught in the lightning of the mercury lamps. Then
they floated far away, very far away: a fat, dwarfish
Germaine; Stopwell as a Louis Philippe armchair
flinging its feet out on both sides. The bar was pitch-
ing. Louise came up with a blurred face like something
out of the artistic film. Her mouth moved, and Jacques
did not hear a single word.

He was no longer luxuriously encased in Germaine.
He could feel his bones, his ribs, his yellow hair, sharp
teeth, freckles, everything he hated and had ceased to
notice.

Below the amplifiers of the waltz which was strang-
ling him, Germaine and Stopwell swept from one end
of the rink to the other on one leg, holding hands, in
the same position as the Auriga. Stopwell threw his
chest out. He thought he was Achilles. For a second
Jacques found him absurd, and naïvely thought that
Germaine would notice it, run away from him, come
back alone, admit that it was a joke.

Louise was not spiteful, but she was a woman. She
remembered. She studied the victim complacently.

Mouheddin came up. Louise winked, pulled a long
face and jerked her chin in the direction of the waltz-
ing couple.

Mouheddin replied to these explanatory gestures
with another which consisted in pushing his lower lip
out and hanging his head, opening his eyes enor-
mously wide.

Jacques' severed head was lolling on his chest.

"Take him home," said Louise to her lover. "He is
going to die."

Jacques refused. He was not the kind to go away.
He belonged to the cursed race that stays to drink the
last drop. The waltz ended. Germaine and Stopwell
returned, catching hold of the chairs and the diners.
Germaine fell over a fat woman. She laughed. The
woman insulted her. Stopwell shrugged his shoulders.
The woman's husband stood up. The woman calmed
him and forced him to sit down again.

Jacques realised there was trouble. None of it
seemed very much to the point.

With the same jerk of the chin, Louise pointed out
the miserable Jacques to Germaine, as if she were
warning a talkative friend at a funeral that he is
standing behind a member of the family.

"He'll get over it," she said. This comment was
humane in the sense that the bullet fired by an officer,

Louise: She studied her victim complacently

from point-blank range, at a wounded man who is still breathing, is an act of mercy in the eyes of the law.

"A cigarette?" Stopwell suggested.

A delightful gesture on the part of the hangman.

*   *   *

Now that the retreat had sounded, they went out. They got into Germaine's car. Hoisted up, tossed about, enfeebled, Jacques saw a confused setting on either side. A profile: Mouheddin; the Odeon, posters, the Luxembourg, the Gambrinus Restaurant, the pool. They were taking Stopwell back.

The car stopped near the Pantheon. Stopwell got out. As Jacques remained seated:

"Come on, are you asleep?" said Germaine. "We're here."

He stammered, jumped out, and went in silently with Stopwell. Mouheddin went home with Louise.

Peter went to his room and Jacques to his. There, falling on his knees at the bedside, he vented his tears, which hung like a liquid lens from his eye-lashes and made his universe look grotesque.

*   *   *

Jacques did not see how he could live, go to bed,

get up, wash, work or go on at all, with this unbelievable agony which seemed as if it could hardly last an
hour.

He excused himself, had no dinner and went to
bed. He was hoping that sleep would declare a truce

*   *   *

Sleep is not at our command. It is a blind fish which
swims up from the depths, a bird which swoops down
on us.

He felt the fish swimming round in a circle, outside
its bounds. The bird folded its wings, perched on the
edge of insomnia, twisted its neck round, smoothed
its feathers, hopped up and down, but did not enter.

Jacques held his breath like a bird-catcher. At length
the bird took wing. flew away, and Jacques was left
fact to face with the impossible.

Impossible. It was impossible. Because of the swiftness of Germaine's love, a swiftness which he had
acquired from her, Jacques could not distinguish any
transition.

From one second to the next, he had seen a face
miles away. He had felt the hand, now limp, which
only yesterday had still sought his own. The eyes that
met his own were examining, not playful.

He kept on telling himself, it's impossible. I am

dreaming. Stopwell looks down on women and the rest is pretence, an Oxford pose. He is a virgin. He winces the moment physical love is mentioned. "That is not done," he says and adds "how can people sleep together?"

Even if Germaine is following up a whim she will meet a blank.

Stopwell distrusts France. On the other side of the channel, his father the parson, his football team, and his regiment are watching him. The alarm will have no sequel.

*   *   *

Suddenly his eyes were overcome with heaviness. His jaw contracted. The bird was in the snare, the fish in the jar. He was asleep.

He is dreaming. He is dreaming that he is not dreaming, and that Stopwell, wearing a Scottish kilt, forces him to believe he is dreaming. Then he is skating, flying. He flies round the rink where trees are growing. Stopwell is trying to humiliate him, telling Germaine that he is dreaming, not really flying. Germaine is skipping along at Stopwell's side with the aid of a parasol. They use the parasol as a parachute. Stopwell's kilt grows very long, with a train.

Accompanied by a church organ, Germaine is singing *The Silent Honorat*. This meaningless title has a meaning in the dream.

Jacques was falling. He landed at the bottom of a hole full of linen. He was awake. He could hear Mouheddin going to bed. So it was morning. He fell asleep again. He was back at the rink, the part he was skating on was revolving. That is why it looked as though Stopwell were skating. He denounced it to Germaine as a trick. She laughed, kissed him. He was happy.

Petitcopain shook him to go and work. He got up and bathed his face in cold water.

*   *   *

One by one, like soldiers at the command, his sleeping memories awoke and lined up. The skating rink memory also came, but it had hardly arrived when the others shrank. It alone grew larger, and became colossal.

A murdered man can live on, ignorant of his wound, as long as the knife is there. When it is pulled out, he bleeds, and his flesh shrivels up.

The cold water drew the knife out of Jacques' wound.

Although Germaine was asleep at this time, he

decided to run to her to be kissed and scolded, to have his wound closed.

*　　　　*　　　　*

When we wake up, it is the animal, the plant in us that thinks. Naked primitive thought. We see a dreadful universe, because we see aright. Soon afterwards we are loaded with the tricks of the intellect. It brings us the playthings that man invents to hide the emptiness. It is then that we think we see aright. We attribute our uneasiness to miasmas of the mind passing from dream to reality.

*　　　　*　　　　*

Jacques was reassured. His work began at 9 o'clock. There he shook Peter's hand. At 10 o'clock he dived into a car, bought flowers on the way and stopped at Germaine's door.

A surprised Josephine opened the door. Germaine was asleep.

"I'll wake her up," he said.

Jacques went in. Transported by her dreams into the past, Germaine wore her old expression. He examined it, and was delighted. He laid the fresh flowers against her cheeks.

She was one of those alert people who wake up quickly.

"It's you!" she said. "You must be crazy to disturb anyone at this hour."

"I couldn't stand it," he replied. "I dreamt you left me. I jumped into a cab."

Germaine had no hesitation in breaking hearts. She felt, as maids do, that a precious thing, when broken, can be stuck together again.

"That was no dream, little man. Keep your bouquet. I am frank. I love Peter and he loves me. You will find plenty more like me. Let me sleep."

She turned to the wall. Jacques lay on the floor and sobbed.

"Look here, this room isn't a hospital," said Germaine. "I loathe men who cry. Go back to the rue de l'Estrapade and work. You don't lead the life of a student preparing for examinations."

Jacques pleaded with her. She had put on the paraffin, the gas mask of those who are no longer in love. She measured Jacques' love by her own affairs. She thought this fit would pass off in a day. She rang.

"Bring M. Jacques a little brandy, Josephine."

She was imitating the dentist who knows that an extraction makes the patient feel sick and upsets him, but that it soon passes off.

Germaine: that was no dream, little man . . .

E

Jacques drank to please her. Josephine stood him up gave him his hat and his cane, and pushed him out, still behaving like the dentist's housemaid. She knows what follows the shock of the operation but has to let in a new patient who is growing restive.

*   *   *

From that moment Jacques' life was blurred like a bicycle wheel after a fall, like a photographic plate when the camera is partly opened.

"Be kind to him, he is suffering," Mme Berlin kept saying to the schoolmaster.

"What from?"

"Never mind. Women can guess certain things."

For she was continuing her romance.

Mouheddin kept on seeing Louise; his comings and goings harrowed Jacques. Their proximity was poor consolation.

Waiting is the most diminishing occupation. It leaves one vacant like a beehive during a swarm, left only with the rudiments of cheerless work. If our frivolous senses disturb it, they are paralysed by the bees of suffering. We must wait, wait, wait; eat mechanically to provide energy for the factory of false sounds, calculations, memories, hopes.

What was Jacques doing? He was waiting.

F   131

What was he waiting for? A miracle. A sign from Germaine, an express letter.

Lying on his bed, his heart twisted like navigators' knots that are loosened or tightened by the movements of the rope, he listened anxiously for the messenger who brought the telegrams upstairs.

He invented noises in the archway and on the stairs. Distant noises died away in the corridor.

Did he go out? He would not dare return. He would ask the caretaker;

"Has an express letter come for me?"

"No, M. Forestier," she would reply.

Then he thought that the caretaker might not have seen the messenger. He counted up to twelve on every stair. In his credulity he fancied that during this procedure the letter could be generated spontaneously on the table.

One morning he received it. *Come to Louise's at 5, I want to talk to you,* wrote Germaine.

He kissed it, folded it, put it away with the short-sighted photograph and was never parted from it, even afterwards.

How could he be patient until 5 o'clock?

He walked round, talked, and went a little way towards killing the time which was to a great extent killing him.

Jea Cocteau

1907 1957

Germaine: you don't lead the life of a
student preparing for examinations.

Stopwell avoided him, only met him at the dining-table. Mouheddin thought he was cured, Mme Berlin thought him heroic. She felt her love affair with Jacques was like that of the duc de Nemours and the princesse de Clèves.

At 4 o'clock Jacques went to the rue Montchanin. There he found the two women. Louise was pretending to polish her nails. Germaine was pacing up and down. She had a hairstyle which revealed her ears, earrings, a new face, a black and beige check suit which Jacques did not know.

"Sit down," she said. "You know my frankness. I am not the kind of woman who makes believe. Stopwell doesn't want . . ." she laid emphasis on it, "does not want us to go together without you knowing and agreeing. I admit I don't know many friends who would behave like that. We are going out to dinner at Enghien tonight. Is it yes or no?"

"Come on . . . my little Jacques," said Louise, and stopped polishing her nails, "come on, a nice gesture."

She was not displeased.

The "nice gesture" infuriated Jacques. He found the strength to reply.

"There are no nice gestures, Louise. Ministers and patronesses are the ones who make nice gestures. I bow. Love cannot be stopped."

*   *   *

There is hope left even on the guillotine, since the law spares the offender if the knife does not work. Jacques still hoped that his magnanimity would touch Germaine, and bring her back to him.

"Shake hands," she said.

He recognized the English handshake.

"Tea?" asked Louise.

"No, Louise . . . no. I am going."

He closed his eyes. Looking at Germaine's dress through his eyelids, he turned her checks red, making them swing slowly over to the right, regain their shape on the left and swing over again.

In the rue de l'Estrapade, Jacques knocked at Stopwell's door.

"Stopwell, she has told me everything," he declared, "she is free."

Did Peter think that she had admitted everything, or was he seizing the opportunity to drive the point home?

"We are gentlemen. You ought to know that I did not suspect there was a woman in Maricelles' room. I heard movements. I thought I should catch Petitcopain."

After these incomprehensible words, Jacques found

himself back in the corridor, just as if he were *it* in
Blind Man's Buff and the others had made him dizzy.

Mouheddin was going out. Jacques stopped him and
interrogated him. He learnt that on Germaine's evening in the rue de l'Estrapade, during the rite of the
clock, Stopwell, informed by Petitcopain, had gone
into Maricelles' room and apologized. Germaine had
kept him, told him that she was waiting for Jacques,
asked him about the number of pupils, the work, and
English schools. Stopwell thought that French schools
did not provide enough sport and asked her if she
went in for sport. She replied that she did not. She
confined herself to roller-skating. She had told him
which was their skating rink.

"I'll hurry away," Stopwell exclaimed, "for I'm
afraid Forestier may come back up. He is touchy, you
know. He would think I came on purpose. Promise
not to tell him that I opened this door."

Jacques remembered his jokes about the Englishman in *Round the World*.

He returned to his room. He had just found a stain
on his brightest memory.

*　　　*　　　*

And this was where we met him at the beginning of
the book. He was bracing himself. He was putting up

137

a resistance. He had become Jacques again; he was looking at himself in the mirror.

A mirror is not Narcissus' pool; there is no plunging into it. Jacques laid his forehead against it and his breath concealed the pale face that he loathed.

*   *   *

Dark glasses or depression dim the colours of the world; but through them we can stare at the sun and death.

So he envisaged suicide without wincing as if it were a luxurious pleasure cruise. These cruises seem unreal. One has to force oneself to make the preparations.

Jacques was afraid of an unworthy end. He pictured the journalist in Venice, green, cheeks bulging. He remembered a suicide at Maisons-Lafitte after the races, on the banks of the Seine, the forehead a pulp, the feet dancing in the eddying water where he was half afloat.

The previous night a doctor, a tenant on the fifth floor, had been deploring the number of deaths due to drugs. He told the story of one of his patients telephoning him at night, almost insane. Her lover whom she thought to be asleep was dead. He had taken an overdose of powder.

The doctor went there, clothed the body and supporting it under the arms, carried it to a cab to an obliging clinic, to save the married woman and kill the scandal that would have attached itself to the name of a well-known industrialist.

*　　　　*　　　　*

Jacques made up his mind.

*　　　　*　　　　*

About 11 o'clock in the morning he went to the skating rink. Deserted, the room had a different atmosphere. The barman was sweeping his bar. Jacques said good morning to him, and, very red in the face, began,

"You know that I never take drugs."

"Yes, M. Jacques," replied the barman, who knew the expression of the novice.

"Have you any? It's for a Russian girl."

The barman went behind his till, peered round to see if they were alone, took a Jeroboam down from the sideboard it decorated, removed the false bottom, and asked,

"How much would you like? Four grammes, twelve grammes?"

"Give me ten grammes."

The barman counted out ten little envelopes at 20 francs each, pocketed the two notes, and advised that the greatest care should be taken.

"Depend on me," said Jacques, and putting the doses in his pocket, he shook hands with him and left the rink.

To get out more quickly, he went across the rink. This rink was his execution block. It strengthened him in his resolution.

He went back calmly like a man who has taken his ticket and sleeper and no longer has to worry about the tiresome details of the journey.

IX

Regardless of class differences, life carries us on all together, in the same train, to death.

It would be wise to sleep until that terminus. But alas, the journey allures us and we take such inordinate interest in what should only be a way of passing the time that on the last day we find it hard to fasten our cases.

The corridor linking the classes only has to bring two souls together secretly and blend them, for the certainty that one of them will get off, that the journey will come to an end, to make the thought of the destination unbearable. They would like long halts in the open country. They look at the door; with the telegraph wires moving by it is like a clumsy harpist working at an arpeggio and beginning it over and over again.

They try to read; someone comes up. They envy

those who at the moment of death fearlessly put their affairs in order, thinking like Socrates of the barber for Phaedo and the cock for Aesculapius.

Too lonely, Jacques had leapt out of the moving train. Or perhaps this diver wanted to rid himself of the human form that suffocated him. He wanted to find the communication cord.

He undressed, wrote a few lines on a pad which he put in an obvious place and undid the packets of powder.

He emptied them out by the corner into an old cigarette box. The contents sparkled like mica.

On his table stood a bottle of whisky, a syphon and a glass, a habit he had caught from Stopwell. He poured out a whisky, mixed in the powder, and drank it in one gulp. Then he went and lay down.

*   *   *

He was invaded from all sides at once. His face hardened. He remembered a similar feeling at the dentist's. With a coated tongue he felt strange teeth set in wood. A cold vapour like ethyl chloride played on his eyes and cheeks. Waves of gooseflesh ran over his limbs, coming to rest around the heart which was beating as if it would break. The waves swept up and down from his toes to the roots of his hair, like the sea when it is too low and keeps taking from one beach to give to another. A mortal cold replaced the waves; it played, spread out, disappeared and re-appeared like the patterns on watered silk.

Jacques felt a weight like cork, like marble, like snow. It was the angel of death completing his task. He lies down on those who are going to die and waits until their attention is ever so slightly distracted, to turn them to stone.

Death has sent him; he might be an ambassador extraordinary, the ones that take the place of their prince at his marriage. So they do it with indifference.

A masseur is no longer affected by the skin of young women. The angel works coldly, cruelly, patiently, until the spasm. Then he flies away.

His victim could feel that he was implacable, like a surgeon administering chloroform, a boa about to eat a gazelle, expanding gradually like a woman with child.

"The man of snow . . . the man of snow . . ." A confused refrain bewitched his hearing. When children want to stay up with the grown-ups at night and fall helplessly asleep, we tell them about the sandman. They awaken when their chins nod on their chests, and come to the surface bewildered.

Jacques heard a voice intoning, "The man of snow

143

. . . of snow . . . of snow . . ." He must not let himself succumb to it, and he floated, head back, with his ears alone immersed in the unknown element. For what the angel did had this terrible quality; being unlimited, it worked above, below, and within. It was not brutal; the angel would rest and begin again with a new vigour.

What a distance between the decision to drown oneself, the action, and the shock it reserves for the system. Many weak men begin to swim when the water has hardly entered their nostrils or if they cannot swim, they improvise it in desperation.

Jacques was overcome with fear. He wanted to pray, fold his hands. They were heavy, immovable.

When your arm has gone to sleep because you have slept on it, it can be revived quickly with soda water; it is animated, ready to obey. Jacques' hand remained inert.

A man in an aeroplane cannot feel the movement. The machine keeps still. Enclosed in helmet and goggles, he sees houses shrinking and spreading, a lifeless town split apart by its river. The town sways or stands like an atlas map against the wall. Suddenly looping the loop, he can see it painted above his head. This movement of the world around the pilots has disturbing effects. The passenger's stomach seems

to fall away. His ears are blocked up. Dizziness cuts
clean across his chest. He may touch down thinking
he is at an altitude of 3,000 feet: he mistakes the
bracken for a forest.

On his bed, Jacques began to confuse his symptoms
with external phenomena. The walls were breathing.
The ticking of the clock came first from the inkwell,
then from the wardrobe. The window was either shut
or wide open on a sky full of stars. The bed slid,
tipped over, was held in unstable equilibrium. It
overbalanced and slowly righted itself again.

Jacques' head grew clearer, although it was humming like a beehive. He saw Tours, his poor mother
opening the telegram, going rigid, his father fastening
their bags.

"This is the end," he thought. "At our death we
see our whole life." But he saw nothing more. His
mother's face changed. It was Germaine. It was Germaine or his mother. Then Germaine alone. He
found it appallingly difficult to remember her. He
got her eyes and mouth mixed up with the eyes and
mouth of an English girl, one of the beasts he had
desired, glimpsed in the Casino at Lucerne. Everything was submerged by an edelweiss. He had a mag-
nifying glass and was studying this tiny star fish of
white velvet which grows in the Alps. He was nine

years old. They missed the train to Geneva because he was making a fuss, wanting them to buy him one.

"Memories . . ." he said to himself. "My memories are coming back to me."

But he was wrong. The performance closed with the edelweiss.

Nocturnal animals hide by day; a fire will drive them out of their holes. At the end of a corrida the audience in the shade and the audience in the sun are mixed; the drug had such tumultuous effects that it mixed Jacques' dark and light sides. He was vaguely aware of some disaster unconnected with the physical drama. He did not remember his wasted love or the dissolute weeks he had spent; he threw them up like a drunkard returning wine that he has forgotten drinking.

*   *   *

Jacques rose. He was losing his bearings. He could see the backs of the cards. He was not conscious of the system he was wrecking but he had a feeling of responsibility. The night of the human body has its nebulae, suns, earths and moons. A mind less subject to sluggish matter could tell how simple is the mechanism of the universe. If it were not, it would break down. It is as simple as a wheel. Our death

146

destroys universes and the universes in our sky are inside a person of alarming size. Does God contain all? Jacques fell back.

Speculations of this extent are common in men who have taken poison. They delude many mediocre men about their intelligence. They imagine they can solve eternal problems.

After a lull, the watered silk, the shivering, the cramp began again. Jacques felt he was losing strength for the fight. He was inundated with sweat. His heart-beats were not strong. He felt them even less because they had recently been too strong. His shoulders were touching the angel above him. He sank down. The water rose above his ears. This phase was endless.

Jacques had stopped resisting.

"There . . . there . . . there . . ." the angel was saying, "you see we are getting there ; . . it's not so painful . . ."

Jacques replied,

"Yes . . . yes . . . it's very easy, very easy . . ." waiting submissively.

At last, like a torpedoed yacht as heavy as a house giving the salute and plunging slantwise into the sea, Jacques went under.

*　　　　　*　　　　　*

He was not dead.

The angel was obeying an unknown countermand.

*   *   *

Petitcopain was coming back from a school dance (his first dance) at 5 o'clock in the morning, and partly to get matches, partly to establish proof of his exploit, he went in Jacques' room, seeing a light under the door.

He saw the apparent corpse, the pad on which Jacques had written, woke Mouheddin, Stopwell, the Berlins, and the doctor on the fifth floor.

They made hot water bottles, poultices. They gave Jacques a rub down. They forced black coffee between his teeth. They opened the window.

Mme Berlin, who thought she was the cause of the suicide, wept bitterly. Berlin put a shawl around her shoulders.

They begin to organize help. They found someone to watch him. At 8 o'clock the doctor affirmed that Jacques was safe.

To what did he owe his life? To a thief. Once again his dark side saved him, but in reverse. The barman had sold him a relatively harmless mixture.

X

His convalescence was long, as he caught jaundice from the poison in his blood. After the jaundice he had symptoms of neuritis in his left leg; they disappeared. He was glad of the sharp pains which were the only things that took his mind off his obsession; medicine admiringly calls them *exquisite*, putting them on a level with illuminations in a missal.

In spite of the seemly disappearance of the long-jump champion, the rue de l'Estrapade aggravated his exhaustion.

When he could be moved, his mother, who was staying in the hotel and had been sitting up with him for thirty days, enlisted the help of Petitcopain, and finally took Jacques away to Touraine.

*　　　　*　　　　*

It was there on a February afternoon, that Jacques awoke, cured of poison and remedies.

The wallpaper of his room depicted an old hunt. The embers of the fire were intense, furry, striped and feline from a distance and dreadful when seen close to, like the form of a tiger. His mother was near the chaise longue, knitting.

Jacques was prolonging his state of numbness. He was pretending to be still asleep. He stopped his memories of childhood from disturbing his new memories. Clumsily, endlessly, he was moving the chessmen: Germaine, Stopwell, Osiris, Jacques Forestier. He corrected his mistakes, worked out impossible moves.

The game wore him out and wasted the little strength he had gained during convalescence. After a few seconds the chess-board went dim; Osiris, Stopwell, Germaine surrounded him. He was beaten, still beaten. Jacques wondered if there was a mistake, if Germaine were not a false image of his desires, tricking them by a resemblance. No. Desire does not deceive us. She did belong to that race.

For there is one race on earth which does not turn back, does not suffer, love or fall ill; a diamond race which cuts through the men of glass. Jacques worshipped the type from afar. It was the first time he had

Memorandum. Miscreant period.

met it. What harm could a Germaine, or a Stopwell, do to each other? But Stopwell could cut Petitcopain to the heart.

A river race too. Petitcopain and Jacques belonged to the race that was drowned. Jacques made a lucky escape. A little longer, and he would have stayed there. In any case what was the use of him escaping? It would only need one of those rivers to flow, one of those stones to sparkle, and he would run into it to his death.

No! No! He would struggle. Willpower changes the lines on our hands. Fate can be diverted by dams. Ulysses tied himself up; he would tie himself up. He would have a home where he could be safe from sirens. It was easy to recognize them. A man only had to stop listening to them credulously to realize the vulgarity of their musical repertoire.

What was a diamond? The son of coal merchants who have grown rich. We should not sacrifice our hopes of happiness to it. Neither to the river nor to the diamond. He would no longer shed tears over soft or hard water.

So Jacques played with words. He thought he was defining a type, closing in on the enemy, looking him in the face, laying the ghost, guarding against a known danger. The words river, diamond, glass, siren are negro fetishes. A description would be better. But what description? The real monster has too many different heads, so many that they hide its body.

Jacques shifted, smiled at his mother. She stood up. She was about to make a delightful mistake, to admit her jealousy.

"Jacques, Jacques my dear, you must stop torturing yourself for a bad woman," she said.

Jacques dropped his decisions all at once. He shrank up, rebelled. Mme Forestier sat down again. He found his card-case on the table, opened it and out of bravado produced Germaine's photograph. What did he see? An actress. He closed his eyes. His harness came back. He hung on to it. His mother forgave him, and, to break the silence,

"You remember Idgi d'Ybreo, at Mürren?"

She was counting her stitches . . .

"Her death in Cairo is announced in the paper."

This time Mme Forestier dropped her work. Jacques fell back. Tears, deep tears, ran down his cheeks.

"Jacques, my angel . . ." she cried, "what's the matter? Jacques!"

She kissed him, wrapped her shawl round him. He sobbed without answering.

He could see a bed. At the bedside stood the god Anubis. He had a dog's head. He was licking a little face, a proud, noble face, already mummified by suffering.

EPILOGUE

By the end of the month, Jacques was fitter than he had been before his illness, the rest being good for people who are highly-strung. He had to take up his work again. It was decided that he should go back to Paris with his mother, they should live there together, and Mme Forestier should give rooms to a tutor. Jacques had suggested this system. He still felt too unsteady to live without support. He knew that his mother and he would be sure to murder each other, but a fixed point of love and respect would enable him to see whenever he was drifting. His own nature was not straight enough to warn him. It yielded and drifted smoothly away.

M. Forestier no longer needed a plumb-line. He gave his wife to his son. He would go and see them in May.

The morning they returned to Paris, Jacques could tell from his regret that he was not arriving alone, how indispensable Mme Forestier's presence would be. He was suffocated. He dared not join the crowd. He was not good at going into the sea. He found it cold and mad.

Mme Forestier had to air the flat, make arrangements with the staff, remove the dust covers and the camphor. Jacques was to meet her at 7 for dinner in town.

The street stimulated his body now that he was well. My eyes are open, he told himself. I am seeing Paris as I used to see Venice. There has to be drama to wake me up.

Then he sank inert again under a chaos of flats, buses, signs, barricades, kiosks, whistles, underground rumbling. He remembered the young men in Balzac who set their foot on the first rung of a golden ladder when they arrived in Paris. He could not get a foothold. He was heavy, floating over the surface of this buoyant city. He was oil on the water; wreckage. He made himself sick at heart.

He had to go and see a possible tutor his father knew, in the rue Réaumur. As it happened, the tutor was not in. Jacques left a card.

Just as he was passing an office of the Bourse, a man came up from below ground level. He recognized Osiris. Osiris coming up from a necropolis beneath a temple, this was the god Osiris, representing the past. Jacques' heart beat violently. He quickened his pace.

"Hey! Jacques! Jacques!"

Nestor was calling him. It was impossible to escape.

"Where are you going in such a hurry? Really! I didn't expect to see you! Germaine said your family was keeping you isolated in the country. Between you and me, I called you a fly-by-night. I wondered whatever we did to you. You made short work of good manners as far as we were concerned."

Jacques stammered that he had been ill, had just come back from Touraine, and was spending a day in Paris.

"A day in Paris? I shan't let you go. Come and have a Vermouth with me."

The Osiris' office was a few yards away in the rue de Richelieu.

While Nestor was opening the door, taking his coat off, finding the Vermouth and the glasses in a cupboard, Jacques saw a recent photograph of Germaine on the mantelpiece. His eyes filled with tears.

"You are well, but you look pale; drink this," said Nestor. "Vermouth does lymphatics good. Do you smoke? No. I have stopped smoking. I am on a diet. Look at my stomach."

He settled down in the leather armchair and crossed his legs, holding his foot with his left hand, his glass with the right.

"Good old Jack! Germaine kept telling me your family had forced you to leave at once, but I wondered

if you were sulking. Do you ever know with Germaine?
She is such a tease. She will be very pleased to hear
that I have seen you. You know our latest craze, our
great favourite? No, of course, you don't know anything. I bet you anything you won't guess. Mouheddin! Yes my dear boy, Mouheddin. Now we swear by
nothing but Mouheddin. Mouheddin is a poet. Mouheddin is handsome. You can see that she doesn't
change."

Jacques did not expect the Arab's name. Nestor
was delighted at his surprise. He clapped his foot and
laughed.

"Fashion changes. I see them come and go, come
and go. Germaine smokes amber-tipped cigarettes, eats
Turkish Delight and burns harem incense. All of
which disgusts me. I am an old fool. Mouheddin is
always right. Note that if I made her take my bazaar
over she wouldn't have it at any price. That's woman.
That's Germaine. I allow her freedom. We won't
change her."

"And Louise?"

"Louise? Germaine has stopped seeing Louise.
That's another story. Can you imagine, Mouheddin
didn't sleep with Louise. It was platonic love. Then
Germaine got Mouheddin from her by some trick, and
so on and so forth. Her poet was captured. In any case

I am not sorry that she doesn't go and see Louise any more. More jiggery-pokery. Just fancy, before Mouheddin everything had to be English. We were sportsmen, we played golf, rode, ate porridge and read *The Times*. You would have died laughing. As England was the order of the day, we had to have an Englishman. We had an Englishman; a very pleasant one too. You know him: Stopwell. Stopwell, the great favourite just after you left. Jacques bows himself out, we must have something new. Are you with me? England lasted thirty-seven days. A week after the English crisis, she discovered your Stopwell. A month after the discovery, I received anonymous letters. 'Germaine is deceiving you' (you know the style) 'she has rooms in the rue Daubigny.' Very well. I don't jib at that. On my way back from the shooting I go to the rue Daubigny. I ring. Someone opens the door. Do you know who I catch? Stopwell. Stopwell and Louise. That's right. Poor Stopwell was as red as a tomato. Louise laughed till she cried. She took the rooms to hide from the prince who was staying in Paris incognito. You see how evil tongues get their information. On my way home, I hesitated. Ought I to tell Germaine? It's a toss-up how she'll take things. She took it as a tragedy. She thought Stopwell was a virgin. She cried. She was losing her mascot, her plaything, her pet, her England.

It was no use me defending Stop, telling her that flesh is weak, that Louise . . . 'It's no good. He's a beast. Men are vile.' Etcetera, etcetera. She wouldn't let Stop set foot in the house again. She shouted that the house was not a dance-hall, that she would live alone on the farm. I've been hearing things, I can tell you."

*   *   *

Jacques listened, quite embarrassed. Quintus Curtius relates how Alexander gradually assimilated the faults of the barbarians through his contact with them. But if Jacques had acquired a card-sharper's sleight of hand through his contact with Germaine, he had lost it. He was no longer the Jacques of *Round the World*. He could not admit to having been so blind. He was like the detective who guesses that the banker's moustache disguises a thief and fingers the grip of his revolver. He wondered whether Osiris was making fun of him, whether he knew, whether he was leading up to a nasty blow.

Nestor went on,

"I'm afraid she's a devil, a real devil, my poor friend. I love her, and as long as she doesn't deceive me that's the main thing."

Jacques spilt the Vermouth on the chair.

"Leave it, leave it, it doesn't matter," said Osiris.

"She needs to be amused. I can't amuse her. I house her, I clothe her, make a fuss of her, but I have the bank. My head's full of settlements. If I were a Stopwell, a Mouheddin, I'd still be keeping donkeys in Egypt."

He stood up. He drummed on the window.

*　　　*　　　*

These words magnified Osiris so greatly in Jacques' eyes that he stepped back to look at him. He wondered if he could only see the base. It was as if an Osiris of granite seated on the top of five tiers of dead men was smiling down from an incalculable height in a sky studded with cyphers.

Osiris cut short the silence.

"There you are," he said; "that's how we stand. That's the full result of the races. I must go out. Will you come with me? Where are you going? I'll drop you in the car."

Nestor picked up his coat and his top hat. No. Jacques recognized the gullible Nestor. His horns were not the horns of Apis the bull.

*　　　*　　　*

In the office outside a young telephonist was stamping envelopes.

"What are you doing, Jules?" asked Osiris. "Are you putting 50 centime stamps on letters for the town?"

"There were no others about, M. Osiris, and I thought . . ."

"You thought wrong; you are dismissed."

Osiris looked inflexible. The employee was trembling.

"Don't argue," shouted Osiris. "Collect your pay. You are dismissed."

The door was slammed.

On the stairs, Jacques recalled the shattered face of the dismissed employee. In the doorway, his mind was made up. On the pavement, he said,

"I'm sorry, M. Osiris, I have a call to make in the rue Réaumur. But do me a favour. For Jules. He cost you one franc. You are unfair. Why did you dismiss him?"

"Why?" (Osiris paused). "Because *that*, my dear Jacques, *that* is something I can avoid."

Then his expression changed and he took affectionate leave of Jacques. The car disappeared.

Alone in the place de la Bourse, Jacques could still hear Osiris' emphatic *that;* he saw the Oriental tugging at the reveres of his coat as he said it, as if he were tweaking someone's ear.

To him the phrase seemed vague, lofty, mysterious. In it he could see the smile of a Colossus once more.

Doubtless it only held a financial meaning, only gave one example of the powerful method of the Osirises, capable of accepting the heaviest losses without a frown, providing that they were inevitable. But Jacques' mind was running on, adding to it.

He decided, whatever happened, to build his character on this phrase, to keep his feet on the ground, to put on a uniform.

I am irresolute in myself, he thought, and *that is something I can avoid.* The rest by the grace of God.

*   *   *

As he was walking round the Bourse for the fourth time, he saw Osiris's ex-employee behind the railings. Jules looked inordinately gay. He was playing prisoner's base with cyclists from the Havas agency.

"Funny place," muttered Jacques.

These were the very words of an angel who visits the world and hides its wings under a glazier's sheet.

He added, "What uniform can I wear to hide my heavy heart? It is too heavy. It will always show."

Jacques felt himself growing gloomy again. He was well aware that to live on earth a man must follow its fashions, and hearts were no longer worn.

EROTICA

Drawings by Jean Cocteau

The majority of drawings in this volume – obsessional, worshipful and sexually explicit – could not be published in Jean Cocteau's lifetime. Before the first publication of *Erotica* in the early 1990s, few of these images had been seen outside France.

Cocteau's models came from a variety of backgrounds. Some were casual pick-ups, others were lovers and friends. Among those represented here are schoolfriends who influenced his sexual development, as well as two of his most famous lovers – the precocious writer Raymond Radiguet and the actor Jean Marais. Cocteau also drew many of his distinguished contemporaries; included here are candid portraits of Picasso, Stravinsky, Nijinsky, Apollinaire, Sarah Bernhardt, Isadora Duncan and Mistinguett, 'Queen of the Paris Music Hall'.

Highly revealing of Cocteau's search for his own personal 'truth', these sensitively drawn and haunting works have taken their place beside the erotica of such artists as Picasso, Modigliani, Schiele and Neizvestny.

'These erotic drawings are replete with Cocteau favourites – well-endowed teenage sailors disporting themselves in a blatantly sexual manner . . . delectable.' – *Gay Times*

'Lavish . . . a fitting tribute to sexual love and a defiant expression of sexual liberty.' – *Him*

'Putting the cock in Cocteau is this new book by the French Renaissance man himself. Long before Tom of Finland, Jean Cocteau was doodling young studs dressed as chefs, sailors and ruffians with dicks like rolling pins and some pretty bad attitudes.' – *Boyz*

ISBN 0 7206 1181 4   £13.95   246mm x 189mm   110pp

OPIUM
The Illustrated Diary of His Cure

According to legend, Jean Cocteau took to opium in 1923 to assuage his grief at the early death of his protégé, the novelist Raymond Radiguet. Written during last months of a detoxification process in 1930, *Opium* is, paradoxically, a work by Cocteau at the height of his powers and trademarked by his unabashed egocentricity and brio. Predating much of the work for which he is best known, *Opium* is now regarded as one of Cocteau's most important works and a major document in the literature of drug addiction in its own right.

In *Opium* Cocteau describes his extraordinary hallucinations and the price his 'perfect hours' came to exact. There are also reminiscences of some of Cocteau's closest friends including the dancer Nijinsky and Marcel Proust as well as revealing insights behind the creation of masterpieces such as *Orphée* and *Les Enfants terribles*.

Illustrated with 28 of Cocteau's own disturbing drawings

'Such diamond precision of utterance has seldom been combined with so wide an aesthetic range.' – Kenneth Tynan

Of all Cocteau's notebooks this is the most striking, and it gains much from his harrowing drawings.' – *The Times*

'His contribution to the great literature of drug addiction is distinguished by the flashes of insight, the capacity to remember, the observation of the miraculous.' – *Daily Telegraph*

ISBN 0 7206 0800 7   £11.50   216mm x 138mm   168pp

LE LIVRE BLANC

Le Livre Blanc, a 'white paper' on homosexual love, was first published anonymously in France by Cocteau's contemporary, Maurice Sachs, and was at once decried by the critics as obscene.

The semi-autobiographical narrative describes a youth's love affairs with a succession of boys and men during the early years of the twentieth century. The young man's self-deceptive attempts to find fulfilment, first through women and then by way of the Church, are movingly conveyed; the book ends with a strong plea for male homosexuality to be accepted without censure.

Illustrated with many drawings and woodcuts by the author.

ISBN 0 7206 1081 8   £8.50   186mm x 123mm   76pp

If you have enjoyed this book you may like to try some of the other Peter Owen paperback reprints listed below. The **Peter Owen Modern Classics** series was launched in 1998 to bring some of our internationally acclaimed authors and their works, first published by Peter Owen in hardback, to a contemporary readership.

To order books or a free catalogue or for further information on these or any other Peter Owen titles, please contact the **Sales Department, Peter Owen Publishers, 73 Kenway Road, London SW5 0RE, UK,** tel: **++ 44 (0)20 7373 5628 or ++ 44 (0)20 7370 6093,** fax: **++ 44 (0)20 7373 6760,** e-mail: **sales@peterowen.com** or visit our website at **www.peterowen.com**

Peter Owen Modern Classics

Guillaume Apollinaire	*Les Onze Mille Verges*	0 7206 1100 8	£9.95
Paul Bowles	*Midnight Mass*	0 7206 1083 4	£9.95
Paul Bowles	*Points in Time*	0 7206 1137 7	£8.50
Paul Bowles	*Their Heads Are Green*	0 7206 1077 X	£9.95
Paul Bowles	*Up Above the World*	0 7206 1087 7	£9.95
Blaise Cendrars	*Dan Yack*	0 7206 1157 1	£9.95
Blaise Cendrars	*The Confessions of Dan Yack*	0 7206 1158 X	£9.95
Blaise Cendrars	*To the End of the World*	0 7206 1097 4	£9.95
Colette	*Duo and Le Toutounier*	0 7206 1069 9	£9.95
Lawrence Durrell	*Pope Joan*	0 7026 1065 6	£9.95
Isabelle Eberhardt	*In the Shadow of Islam*	0 7026 1191 1	£9.95
Shusaku Endo	*The Samurai*	0 7206 1185 7	£9.95
Shusaku Endo	*Wonderful Fool*	0 7206 1080 X	£9.95
Jean Giono	*Two Riders of the Storm*	0 7206 1159 8	£9.95
Hermann Hesse	*Demian*	0 7206 1130 X	£9.95
Hermann Hesse	*Gertrude*	0 7206 1169 5	£9.95
Hermann Hesse	*Journey to the East*	0 7206 1131 8	£8.50
Hermann Hesse	*Narcissus and Goldmund*	0 7206 1102 4	£12.50
Hermann Hesse	*Peter Camenzind*	0 7206 1168 7	£9.95
Hermann Hesse	*The Prodigy*	0 7206 1174 1	£9.95

Anna Kavan	*Asylum Piece*	0 7206 1123 7	£9.95
Anna Kavan	*The Parson*	0 7206 1140 7	£8.95
Anna Kavan	*Sleep Has His House*	0 7206 1129 6	£9.95
Anna Kavan	*Who Are You?*	0 7206 1150 4	£8.95
Yukio Mishima	*Confessions of a Mask*	0 7206 1031 1	£11.95
Anaïs Nin	*Children of the Albatross*	0 7206 1165 2	£9.95
Anaïs Nin	*Collages*	0 7206 1145 8	£9.95
Anaïs Nin	*The Four-Chambered Heart*	0 7206 1155 5	£9.95
Anaïs Nin	*Ladders to Fire*	0 7206 1162 8	£9.95
Boris Pasternak	*The Last Summer*	0 7206 1099 0	£8.50
Cesare Pavese	*The Devil in the Hills*	0 7206 1118 0	£9.95
Cesare Pavese	*The Moon and the Bonfire*	0 7206 1119 9	£9.95
Mervyn Peake	*A Book of Nonsense*	0 7206 1163 6	£7.95
Edith Piaf	*My Life*	0 7206 1111 3	£9.95
Marcel Proust	*Pleasures and Regrets*	0 7206 1110 5	£9.95
Joseph Roth	*Flight Without End*	0 7206 1068 0	£9.95
Joseph Roth	*The Silent Prophet*	0 7206 1135 0	£9.95
Joseph Roth	*Weights and Measures*	0 7206 1136 9	£9.95
Cora Sandel	*Alberta and Jacob*	0 7206 1184 9	£9.95
Natsume Sōseki	*The Three-Cornered World*	0 7206 1156 3	£9.95
Bram Stoker	*Midnight Tales*	0 7206 1134 2	£9.95
Tarjei Vesaas	*The Birds*	0 7206 1143 1	£9.95
Tarjei Vesaas	*The Ice Palace*	0 7206 1122 9	£9.95
Tarjei Vesaas	*Spring Night*	0 7206 1189 X	£9.95
Noel Virtue	*The Redemption of Elsdon Bird*	0 7206 1166 0	£8.95